TRIGGER WARNING

The following work of fiction is intended for an immature audience. If you are easily offended by words or fail to understand satire, please put the book down and report to the nearest groupthink safe space.

But don't return the book for a refund. Let's not do anything crazy.

1

Chad's Diorama

The eyes open. His eyes. My eyes. There is no difference, we're one and the same. What he saw, I see. Unified perception.

It's a beach somewhere. A private beach. Maybe Bora-Bora or that cheap knock off in the Philippines. No, either Bora Bora or someplace even more exclusive. Some place us worker ants don't even know about. After all, this is not the type of man who cares about price tags.

I'm lying comfortably in a wooden beach recliner, close to the pearl white sand. It's almost surreal how perfect the scene is. The white sands and crystal-clear water. The sounds of the crashing waves and birds calling somewhere outside my field of view. The fresh sea breeze rushing past me. This truly is paradise. If only I could afford the real thing.

I let myself get carried away, for a moment trying my best to ignore the fact none of this is real. Someone's touch on my right startles me. I turn and see fingers running gently down my arm. I follow them and find this stunning blonde girl in a light blue bikini. She's got to be a model or at least a high-end escort. The type of escort whose company costs more per hour than the average car. Totally worth every cent, though. She closes her eyes and giggles with a cute smile then runs towards the water, visibly excited. But I don't follow her. I stay there in the beach recliner and sip some beer. Even the taste of it is unfamiliar. Hetap brand. One of those thousand-dollar reserve bottles.

She gets in the water and plays around for a bit. Splashing herself, she calls for me but I stay in the chair, sipping some more beer. Then I see it in her face, but only for an instant. She's hurt I'm not giving her attention. Or maybe she doubts her ability to satisfy a customer. Maybe she doesn't realize this guy is used to snorting coke off the ass of one like her or better every night. Sometimes maybe two or three. The sky's the limit when you're a celebrity billionaire. She smiles again. It wouldn't be a good thing to receive unfavorable reviews in her line of work.

I recline back and stare at the sky for a few minutes. One could only guess what was going through his mind at that moment. Boredom, I think. The poor tortured soul has seen so much, experienced so much. Fucked so many. There is no novelty left in the world for him. Oh, boo-hoo. Cry me a river, plutocrat.

"Hey," I hear her voice, as sweet as I had imagined. A singer's voice. Carefully modulated to seduce. Maybe a singer whose career never picked up. Without friends in the right places, it's prostitution for you, sweet girl.

I look down and see her standing a few feet away, soaked in seawater, her sky-blue eyes locked with mine. She smiles slyly then turns around and takes off her bikini top. I nod and take a sip. Still facing away, she does a little dance and undoes the laces keeping the bottoms in place. I don't react much beyond taking a sip.

She gets it. This escort or prostitute or whatever, knowing this is her chance at stardom. A once in a lifetime chance to fuck someone already rich and famous. If she does it right, she might get a piece of the pie. Won't be the first time. Play your cards right, girl, and you might get your own rama channel.

The dancing doesn't go on for much longer when she seems to decide it's been enough teasing and climbs on me. We kiss while my hands go exploring that perfectly smooth skin of hers and she fakes little moans here and there. I know what happens after this. It's always the same.

Arias... Brezer... I start in my head, focusing as hard as I can through the mental noise of the diorama. *Ceres...*

The scene comes to a standstill then fades to nothingness as the forced dream ends and I wake up inhaling deeply then exhaling. Sleep paralysis goes away after a few seconds and I remove the diorama visor off my head and toss it aside. I sit up on the edge of the capsule, still a little disoriented. Eventually my mind returns to clarity and the loud pop music playing inside Azim's Rama arcade helps pull me back to reality.

"You interrupt! Why do you interrupt?" Azim shouts from a distance. I have to rub my eyes to see what's going on. Other customers in pods around me lie there, visor over their eyes, lost in whatever fantasy they paid for. I notice a wet spot on the crotch of the guy dreaming in the pod next to mine. He'll be done soon. I wish I hadn't seen or smelled that.

"No refunds!" exclaims Azim with his thick Arabic accent. I sit on the edge of the pod still fighting some leftover disorientation and look up to see the Egyptian immigrant. As usual, I wonder why he wears the stereotypical Muslim long shirt and little hat in LA like we're in the middle of the god damn desert.

Against the wall, a sign with big stylized lettering reads:

Remember the Cancel-Out Safe Words!
Arias-Brezer-Ceres
Easy as A-B-C!

5

"I know, I know," I drunkenly say, getting off the pod but still leaning on it while I regain my balance.

"Listen, friend," says Azim with that deep loud voice that demands attention over the other noises in the arcade, "you stop at the best part!"

"It's boring."

"Boring?" he asks with a wide misshapen grin. Azim could really use some time alone with an orthodontist. "What you mean boring? You don't like tits?"

I chuckle and shake my head. "Porn, it's always the same. It gets old."

"Ah, I see, my friend," he continues but lowers his voice, sly smile on his face. "I got some exotic ramas in the back. What do you want? Boy? Girl? Age is just a number, I don't judge!"

"Nah, I'm done for tonight," I say and rub my eyes again as I look for the exit.

"What do you mean done? I got dioramas! Thai, Japanese, Latina, very exotic!"

"Thanks," I say with a smile and walk away.

"Eh! Typical American and your pretend disgust for sex," says Azim and walks back to his control station in the middle of the room.

I shrug and look around his fine rama establishment. Most of the pods against the circular wall are occupied. The subtle but distinct smell of fresh semen floats in the air, lightly masked by air fresheners plugged at strategic places along the wall. Makes me wonder just how many customers Azim gets on average. Maybe I should open my own arcade. Regardless of the crash, the one reliable constant of showbiz will never go away. Sex sells. A lot.

I open the door and step out. It's dark already but the huge neon sign of Azim's Rama lights up the street much better than the aging street lamps above. I cover my nose and make my way home. I've left the faint scent of cum behind but out here, its piss and shit and a cloud of bodily odors that waft out of the Pershing Square tent city. Fuck, I hate summer. Makes Downtown Los Angeles stink more so than usual. Chad Mars. The name runs through my mind. A minor heir of some banking empire turned rama celebrity. Capturing his experiences living the billionaire high life then making the stupid masses his family controls pay for the privilege of dreaming them in diorama form. And all he had to do was pop out of the right cunt. The lucky bastard.

My place is 3 blocks away. I could have ridden the bike but I like these walks outside, especially in these damn heat waves. It's close to 9:00 PM. Helps clear the mind to disconnect from it all. Silent cars zip past me, leaving behind their characteristic mist of ionized water and other byproducts of hydrogen synthesis that mask the sour stench of the city for a few seconds.

Rows of homeless people lie on the sidewalk. Some sleeping. Others getting high. But most of them lost in some rama or another, wearing those shitty portable diorama visors volunteers pass around. I wonder how much the 'non-profit' who sells them to the City makes for each one. Probably cheaper than drug rehabilitation. Got to keep my eyes on the ground, watch for discarded needles. Can't get pricked with one of those. Good luck explaining to people that's how you got AIDS and not by taking dicks up the ass or something.

My building is one of those that used to lease cuck boxes for $10k a month. Totally worth the privilege of a 900xx zip code for the trust fund babies and Hollywood hopefuls. Thank God the crash got rid of the lot. It still got some luxuries but the place is mostly empty. I climb the stairs to the second floor. When I get there, the proximity key unlocks the door to my little fortress of solitude. It's still a cuck box but at least decently priced and a short walk away from work.

Step in. Turn on the AC. Wake up my computer. Put wallet, keys and phone on the desk. Get a beer from the

7

fridge. Sit down in front of the computer. Open the browser. Click on the TorChan shortcut. Amuse myself with the rants of social outcasts, pseudo-intellectuals, armchair sociologists and over-analysts for an hour. Maybe two. Just like most evenings. This time, I notice a thread about Chad Mars and lurk for a little bit. Half the anons praise his rugged manliness. The other half points out the unfair benefits of having everything handed to him on a silver platter from birth. I reply to one of those. I defend the billionaire and call the haters 'commies.' Couldn't give two shits about Chad Mars but anon's reaction to trolling never fails to amuse. I get my quick, cheap dopamine rush, and then a sip of beer. The cheap stuff. Maybe I'll save up a few month's salary and buy a bottle of that Hetap stuff Mr. Mars was indulging in his lavish vacation.

But then I realize. The beer was a native ad embedded in the diorama. Fuck, they almost got me.

2

Promoting Synergy

Dreamax. A subsidiary of Tarios Group, one of those ambiguously named Saudi investment conglomerates. One of the few entertainment companies still trying real hard to make the old Hollywood formula work for rama production, marketing and distribution. Trying real hard and failing. Must suck being a marketing slave in here. How do you even advertise dioramas? Not that I'm complaining. Pays the bills and even if Dreamax crashes and burns, plenty of other companies are always hiring IT guys.

I like my desk. It faces a window with a nice view of Downtown LA and beyond. At least from the 3rd floor you don't see the tent cities or condemned buildings full of junkies, that is if you look straight ahead. The water cooler is right next to my cube so I can overhear the slaves talk about fantasy football, hiking trips, the game last night, the latest zany concoction at Starbucks or whatever other fascinating politically correct HR-approved conversation topics they engage in. I like how it's right next to the staircase access door too. I can come and go and rarely bump into a slave.

It's a regular Monday. Trouble tickets start to pile up in the system. Slaves complaining about a harmless pop-up here or a PDF reader update there. Slaves pinging me in chat complaining their computer is slow.

'Please open a ticket and the next available help desk team member will follow up when they reach it in the queue.' Standard reply. I have it macroed to my keyboard. I can do things with information systems the slaves can barely comprehend but I'm still distracted by someone's PDF reader acting up. I guess to them once an IT guy, always an IT guy.

"Hey bro, did you watch the game last night?" A head pops on the side of my cube.

"Dave, good morning," I look up, away from my screen to return the greeting with a smile. Apparently there was a game last night. Sunday night football? Is there a World Cup going on?

"So, did you watch it?" He insists.

"Dude, do I look like I care about sports?" I reply, pointing at my size 46 waist. Standard reply, macroed in my head.

He chuckles. I chuckle too. Must be friendly to the slaves. Must promote interdepartmental synergy and all that.

"Say, my PDF reader is doing this weird thing where it..." There he goes. Pretend greeting before getting to the point. I barely pay attention to the complaint but still smile and nod.

"Don't worry, Dave. Open a ticket and someone from help desk will get to it on the double." Standard reply, etcetera.

He looks down. I see a hint of confusion in his face. Dave, all-American specimen. Mid-20s or early 30s. Tall, perfectly combed hair, well-ironed suit. Popular. Probably used to all kinds of doors opening for him with little else than a simple smile. Sales type of guy all around. But it's not my job to care about his PDF reader troubles.

"Yeah, I'll do that," Dave says and he walks away.

I stand up and take a peek at the help desk guys in the open office bullpen. Eric talks to Dave. He'll rescue him from his PDF reader troubles. Mia is on the phone. She remote supports someone. Rich is just sitting there playing Minecraft. Who the fuck still plays Minecraft anymore? I sit back down and continue trying to figure out why this stupid diorama clip keeps failing mastering.

Save for the usual slaves who assume all sysadmins do is fix PDF Reader, it can be a fun job, playing with expensive information systems equipment and getting paid for it. Most days come and go so fast I don't realize months pass me by. It's Independence Day next week. Another year halfway gone.

It's time for a break. On my screen, I bring up the Dreamax Intranet to look at the dreamer intake schedule and right there, almost as if by destiny, ToBogan in the house. I stand up and leave my cubicle. Let the help desk guys deal with PDF Reader. Got better shit to do.

It's a small office, Dreamax headquarters. It doesn't take long to go from IT to Pre-Production. Open office. No privacy. Promotes collaboration, Linda from HR says. Promotes synergy. Promotes saving the boss man money on real furniture, I think. I walk past the HR office. Linda and Maria sit inside. Soccer moms. Better not even peek inside and spare a sexual harassment accusation. They have inspirational posters inside. 'Think like an entrepreneur,' one reads. More like 'work 16 hours a day and expect nothing in return, slave,' I think.

I take the elevator down to the shops. As soon as it dings and the doors open, I can hear the Aussie legend and steroids enthusiast tell stories surrounding his latest rama capture trip.

"...oh yeah mate? You try havin' a naughty 'nder the outback sun, sweaty, stinky fanny and all..." he loudly says. One of those loud guys who speaks in ALL CAPS IRL.

I can barely tell what the hell's he's going on about half of the time. He stands there in the middle of the catch shop, blathering away about some sexual adventure in the Australian outback. I look around and I see the guys laughing and the few girls in the room, I can categorize into two groups. The ones that look around embarrassed and the rest who bite their lips and give him bedroom eyes. He's one of the few studio dreamers whose ramas still draw paying customers and so he can act any way he damn pleases, which makes him a pretty cool guy in my book. One wonders how many HR complaints were conveniently ignored for the sake of rama stream revenue.

"Oi! Teddy, mate," he shouts enthusiastically as he sees me. "How you doing you fucking nerd!?"

"I'm doing alright, Topher. Thanks for asking."

"This fucking guy right here," he says, as he comes closer and runs his arm on my shoulders, addressing the room but no one in particular. "This guy always knows where in the outback I am. Fuck, he knows the mating habits of the critters I molest in my ramas."

"Well, you know me," I say a little embarrassed at being put in the spotlight, but at the same time appreciating the call out. "I like to read."

"Nah, that's not it. Smart fucker right here," he says, pointing at my head with his free hand.

The man. ToBogan. Eventually he lets go and continues shaking hands and high-fiving the techs. Topher Bass, the rama sensation. The Top Bogan. The Maximum Straya. Or at least that's how he called himself back when he was making a name in RamaHub. Nowadays he must dream family-oriented, politically correct, advertiser friendly ramas. A sellout, basically. Still like the guy. I envy the guy. The ease with which he can relate to others. To present himself wide open with zero defenses, completely as he is. Not an ounce of the plastic fakeness you see in people all over the place in LA. No fear. No doubt. Pure confidence.

Maybe I can learn something from this true alpha.

He continues towards the back of the shops and I follow him to the dreamcatchers. The Maximum Straya is scheduled for rama intake with Scott. A technician out of many who tends to the dreamers. They meet by Scott's dreamcatcher and exchange greetings. ToBogan remembers the names of Scott's kids and their ages. How the fuck he does that still eludes me.

"Hey Scott," I wave to the technician.

"What's up Ted? Checking out another intake?"

"Yeah," I say with a grin. "I want to steal your job at some point. Teach me your secrets."

"No secrets here, friend. Anything I know I'll share," he says returning the grin.

Scott shows ToBogan to his dreamcatcher. It's a long chair with a device built into the headrest. The Straya lays down and takes a long deep breath then exhales slowly.

"Ready when you are, mate," says ToBogan.

Scott nods and checks the chair here and there. Safety checks. I've seen videos online of what happens when a dreamcatcher malfunctions. Not a pretty sight. He seems to be done making sure he won't lobotomize the Aussie legend then sits down at a workstation next to the chair. ToBogan gives Scott a thumbs up and Scott types something on his keyboard.

"Alright, big guy," says Scott. "You know the drill. Relax your body and focus your mind. Give me a nice, clear entry point."

I stand behind Scott and watch his workstation monitor. A diagram of a brain and a completion bar underneath show up. Progress notices come up as the catch moves on from one stage to the next.

Scanning for Memory Entry   Point...

Possible Match Found!

"Attaboy Topher," says Scott and then he turns on a dial on his fancy control station. There are dials and levers and buttons that make it look like the controls of a starship.

ToBogan clenches his teeth and closes his eyes, taking in the migraine inflicted by rama catching. I see a small tear run out of his right eye. Single manly tear. It's fascinating to behold such an alpha specimen of manhood be reduced to tears. Not to mention the long-term effects of catching ramas out of one's brain. But the Maximum Straya endures and the catch goes on.

Diorama Located!

Catching Diorama...

A little label under the status notice shows a percentage counter starting from zero and progressing a unit about every 10 seconds. That's gonna take a while. ToBogan holds on to the armrests for dear life and I feel the distinctive vibration of my phone in my pocket. I pull it out and read a new text message.

From: Lucy
Hey

I push the lock screen button and pocket the phone back. The catching process continues.

"Hey Scott, you ever catch something you shouldn't be looking at?" I ask the tech.

"Dude, all the time," he replies with a grin. "But by labor law we're not supposed to immerse into any dioramas until ToBogan here dreams the whole raw sequence back and signs a statement giving Dreamax ownership of it, private or not."

"So you have to do all this again until the right rama

comes up?"

"An amateur dreamer might have trouble giving us an entry point for the catch, but experienced pros like ToBogan over here are usually good on the first try."

ToBogan struggles to open his eyes and through the pain raises the right arm to give me a thumbs-up. The whole scene reminds me of a creepy old school movie where a mental patient is given electro shock therapy. I return double thumbs-ups with both hands.

"Cool," I say to Scott.

"You know, if you want to learn more about the technical details of diorama catching, there are some free training materials online," Scott says. He's a nice guy. Team player. HR poster boy. "You don't have to listen to my lectures if you want to transfer to the shop."

"Nah, it's cool. It's more curiosity of mine rather than professional interest," I lie.

Scott shrugs and continues the catch. I stay behind him and watch which buttons he pushes and dials he turns and levers he pulls. I look around the shop and people going about their workdays. There are several dreamcatchers around but only the one ToBogan is sitting in is being used. I feel the text message vibration of my phone again and pull it out.

From: Lucy
Hey
I got some new stuff. Dark web stuff.
You'll like it.

Probably bootleg ramas. I lock and pocket the phone again. Some minutes go by and eventually the ordeal for ToBogan is done. Scott powers down the dreamcatcher and the Straya gets up and turns away from us to wipe tears from his eyes. Can't let the betas ever see alpha tears. The betas might see weakness. The betas might attempt to challenge him for alpha-dom.

"You okay, buddy?" asks Scott, as he taps the Straya's shoulder.

"Yeah, yeah. Standard procedure, mate. No biggie," ToBogan replies.

"Excellent. I'll run some garbage cleanup then you'll be able to certify the rama in a couple of hours."

"Yeah, I know the drill," ToBogan says and looks around the room, not near as loud as he was before. "Gonna use the toilet real quick."

Scott nods and sits back down at this workstation to do his thing. My phone shakes again. It's like she doesn't get the message. I pull it out and notice Scott pulls out his too. It's not Lucy this time. It's the Dreamax HR app, showing a notification inviting all staff to the bleachers. I look at Scott who looks back at me after checking his own notification then shrugs to let me know he doesn't know what the impromptu gathering is about either.

"Well, wanna go check it out?" I ask.

"Yeah in a minute, I have to finish some things here," he says. Can't walk the hallowed halls of Dreamax with an IT guy I guess. I nod and make my way to the break room. Who knows how long the meeting is going to be. Better grab a drink. I see the slaves hurrying to the meeting. Don't want to be the last ones to the bleachers. Don't want our fearless leader to see them get there last. I grab a mineral water, swipe my credit card on the automated cashier's reader and continue to the main hall.

Dreamax HQ is a three-story building. The basement and ground floor is where the shops are. Where the actual work is done. Dreamers come in and the techs catch dioramas, which then go to cleanup, post-production, editing and all that. The final product is then formatted for a variety of rama player brands and encoded with our proprietary DRM shit. The DRM usually stops hackers for a couple weeks which is the really short window any rama studio has to make money.

After that, most people just pirate the shit out of them. One reason out of many only an idiot would go on business to sell studio ramas nowadays.

The second floor is where the money sinks are. IT, HR, Finance. Without us in the second floor, any work done by anyone else in the company would grind to a halt. But still, we're not sexy like Sales or Marketing. No, we're cost centers and so we rarely see budget or perks. We're money sinks and not much else.

Third floor are Sales, Marketing, Talent and Executives. The good-looking people. The Hollywood people. The bros walking around with protein shakes, talking about the game last night. The girls posting pictures of their lunch on social media or whatever other frivolous vapid bullshit they engage in with their sorority sisters. These are the smooth talkers and smilers and social media picture-perfect, well-aligned teeth, gym members, ivy league graduates, well-connected, highly functional, above average individuals. Or at least that's the image they obsessively portray in their half-dozen social media accounts. One can only guess what really goes on behind closed doors for the members of the Adderall fan club.

I open my mineral water and take a sip. I love mineral water. It feels like drinking flavorless tooth paste. Eventually, I make it to the bleachers and find slaves are still finding a place to sit down while our fearless leader, CEO Audrey Reynolds holds a microphone and does that CEO thing where she spots random people in the crowd and points and calls their name. The slaves eat this kind of shit.

'Oh, look she knows my name. This important, genetically superior, captain of industry and leader of the community still finds space in her brain to squeeze my name in. Surely I'm that important to her and the company. Surely being a good corporate boy pays off. I bet Stacy from Accounting is super jealous of me right now. I should post this moment in the sosh nets!'

That's got to be what goes through a slave's brain when a CEO points at them and calls their name. I do wonder where that practice came from though. Maybe they teach that in ivy league business school. When you go through business leader training, they probably have a class on how to act like a lower-tier human being to establish some sort of connection. Some sort of relatability with the troops. Must promote team synergy and all that.

Audrey continues her round of smiles and pointing and name-calling with the occasional hand shake here and there. The bleachers area is this wooden structure near the front door that looks like oversized stair steps. Sometimes we use it for meetings, others for announcements. Last year we watched the Trump/Ocasio-Cortez presidential debates here with beers and sliders. That was fun.

"Alright guys, let's settle dooooowwwwwwn," says Linda from HR with her annoying vocal fry, as usual playing bad cop for corporate when an order has to be relayed to the slaves. Execs can't look condescending or like they're giving orders. No, that's a job for HR so they're used for deflection or to prevent workplace lawsuits. Fuck, I love corporate America.

The noise dies down. I sit next to Sophie from Legal. Cute, petite girl. I wonder how someone like that holds their ground in court. I wave to Steve Kowalski, my boss, who waves back and sits two levels up. Linda greets us and apologizes for interrupting our workdays with an unplanned, impromptu meeting. She goes on about HR reminders. Sign up for the company spin class, fill up the online poll, take your yearly sexual harassment sensitivity training, but that one only applies to male slaves. We all know only us males have to constantly keep our inherent rapey tendencies under control while female employees are pure, elevated beings with none an impure thought to besmirch their characters.

Eventually Linda shuts up and concedes the stage to our fearless leader.

"Good morning, Dreamaxers!" exclaims CEO Audrey Reynolds who receives thunderous applause in return. "Thank God it's Monday! Like Linda said, our apologies for pulling you out of the zone, but we have exciting news to share..."

This can't be good. She goes on and on about positive things in the industry and our company. Probably softening the blow that is incoming.

"... but as we all know, all around the studio diorama industry we see trouble..." here we go. "Sony shut down their entertainment division last year. An entire, well-established titan of entertainment spaces shut down their music, videogame, motion picture, virtual reality and diorama divisions all at once. This is very scary stuff."

Now she's doing that thing where we're reminded how badly our competitors are doing so whatever is going to happen to us we shouldn't feel so bad.

"... and it's admirable. I have nothing but respect for our team." Pause for dramatic effect. "We have prevailed where others have failed and every single one of you should be proud of such an achievement. We are winners, all of us in this room. But..."

But. There's always a 'but.' Here it comes.

"... as you all know, diorama sales are down. Studios struggle to produce the types of content that most strongly engage our audiences..."

You mean porn, small animal torture or pranks that involve property damage among other fine genres. Yeah good luck having any studio rama go viral the way a Chad Mars indie rama does. The MBAs don't get it. These MBAs employed by bankers and investors who think there can be a rama 'industry' the way Hollywood was. I feel sorry for CEO Audrey Reynolds. Heiress to a Hollywood empire who came of age just as the entire movie industry collapsed. Then the major studios shut down one by one and the entertainment economy that sustained Los Angeles crashed.

Hard. The money people fled LA like rats. Took all the money with them. Took all the investment. Hell, even Silicon Valley titans ran away to states where they wouldn't be taxed to extinction. Then to top it all out, a dirty bomb goes off in the port of San Pedro and the whole area has to be cordoned out due to radiation and shipping traffic gets diverted elsewhere. Now California has fallen from its high pedestal. Now LA is what Detroit was in the 80's. At least real estate is not the obscene bullshit it was at its peak.

She keeps trying though, with the help of unwise foreign investments. Saudi Kings, Chinese officials of The Party and whoever else still romanticizes Hollywood when the rest of the world has moved on. No one gives a shit about music, movies, videogames or VR anymore. It's all about the ramas now. Not even clean, studio produced ramas but the indie stuff. Complete unaltered creative freedom for the dreamers, even if that means sometimes shit gets dark. But that's why they're viral. The drones at large love it when shit gets dark. The desensitized masses who spent their childhoods consuming healthy doses of ISIS beheading videos and all kinds of readily available porn, legal and otherwise. No, the masses don't care about your diorama documentary about the rivers of Utah. No, the masses want to dream about rape, murder, drug use and whatnot, and this is why your company is dying. This is why your family fortune is being wasted. People like you made it so it was impossible to make money in entertainment unless your content was as family and advertiser friendly as possible. Clean, sterilized, shiny and devoid of any humanity but immune to the PR nightmares caused by social justice warriors bitching on Twitter about how the latest movie or rama is not diverse enough.

And this is why Dreamax will fail, just like all other diorama studios. Ironic, really.

"… but we'll get through this." Pause for dramatic effect as she looks up and down the bleachers. "We'll get through it with teamwork, quality and doing our best, as we've always done it even if sometimes we have to do more with less..."

More with less. CEO speak for cutbacks. Maybe layoffs. Oh boy here we go. Audrey stops talking and cedes the floor back to Linda from HR.

"There have been rumors about cutbaaaaaaacks for the last few weeeeeeks and today we're sad to confirm this is indeed the caaaaaase. After this meeting, we'll do a manager's and up catch-up to discuss executioooooooon. Sadly, some of you will be moving on to other opportunities beyond Dreamaaaaaaax."

Fuck. Time to update my resume I guess. Linda from HR continues apologizing about a corporate strategy that makes complete sense. I've never taken it personal when a company downsizes. I certainly hope the slaves don't either. Maybe I'll land a job in medical IT. People may no longer watch movies or dream studio ramas but they still get sick and die all the time. Job security for years to come.

My phone vibrates again and I decide to check the notification rather to listen to the vocal frayed apologies of Linda from HR. It's another text message from Lucy.

> From: Lucy
> Hey
> I got some new stuff. Dark web
> stuff. You'll like it.
> Come check it out tonight
>
> To: Lucy
> Okay

Yeah, I'll go see my ex tonight. Why not? It's not like the TorChan anons will miss me.

3

Hardware and Software

Lucy's apartment is in North Hollywood. A few years back, trying to drive from Downtown up here at rush hour would be bumper to bumper hell on the 101 during a window that spanned 4 or 5 hours in the afternoon. Nowadays the ride takes about 15 minutes.

If Downtown LA is a literal shithole taken over by homeless tent cities, North Hollywood is even worse, but for its own reasons. The celebrities, executives and upper managers who could afford to get out, got out. Real estate values plummeted and the houses they left behind were purchased by mid-level Mexican cartel lieutenants or wealthy Chinese immigrants. Nowadays it's sort of an unofficial red district. This is the place to come if you want to grab a hooker or some coke. Or if your ex-girlfriend sends you cryptic text messages bugging you to come visit.

The streets are littered with trash. Storefronts that years ago were used by small quaint businesses are now adult-only rama arcades or poorly concealed brothels. There are 'massage parlors' here and there where girls wearing nothing but a doctor's robe stand on the sidewalk passing out flyers. 'Open from 6:00 PM to 3:00 AM, $200 an hour.' Seems legit. My guess is they bring much needed tax revenue or someone in City Hall is either in a cartel's payroll or intimidated into looking the other way. Convenience stores make bank in this sort of neighborhood. Open 24/7, selling condoms, snacks, needles, drinks, alcohol. If opening a rama arcade doesn't happen for me, one of those would be an acceptable second option.

I arrive at the apartment building but can't find a parking space for another couple blocks. My somewhat late-model car stands out from the pieces of junk parked next to it. I hope its alarm system works as advertised. Even after police departments through the state lost a lot of funding, California is still a may-issue state but for all intents and purposes, getting a gun conceal carry permit is near impossible. Two blocks walk in near complete darkness in a neighborhood controlled by cartel gangs. Whatever she's got, better be worth it.

Somehow I make it in one piece to the front door of her building. I push the button for her apartment in the comms console but nothing happens. The stupid thing is broken. Out of frustration I lightly punch the door and it just opens wide for me. Talk about safety. I walk in. It's one of those apartment buildings with three levels, stairs going up in the corners and a pool in the middle. The pool is empty save for the deep end where I see a foot or so of disgusting greenish rain water. Someone's playing loud hip hop music. Someone else competes with Mexican narco-corridos. Shitty people engaged in a shitty competition for dominance of the nearby airwaves by means of shitty music. And everyone else caught in the crossfire are just collateral damage. I walk up the stairs all the way to the third level. My plump physique is not accustomed to this kind of activity so I hyperventilate, eventually making it there feeling like I'm about to drop dead from a heart attack. Her apartment door is right next to the staircase but I hold on to the handrail and take a minute to recover my stamina. I feel better now, let's go visit Lucy. I walk up to the door and knock a couple times. Nothing. Could be she gave up waiting on me and went to bed. Nah, it's only a little bit past 7 and this is Lucy. She probably goes to sleep at sunrise after a night of lurking the interwebs.

I knock again. Nothing. But then I hear her voice from inside saying "hold on!"

That's fine Lucy, take your time. She's probably putting on pants or something. The door opens and the noise of computer equipment inside escapes. And there she is, my ex-girlfriend. Shorter than me. Average body. Black hair cut short. Just as socially retarded and running on junk food as me but somehow keeping herself several pounds safe from obesity. She's got these big brown eyes that make you feel as if she can see right through you. They remind me why at some point it felt like I was in love with her but also why we drifted apart. To this day it still baffles me why she went out with me in the first place. Not to mention insisting on keeping in touch after the break up.

"Well you're going to stand out there all night or what?" she asks then turns to get back inside. I grunt in lieu of articulating a proper response like a human being with minimal social skills would and follow her.

"So, how you been?" I ask. She shrugs and sits in a fancy multicolored leather 'gaming' chair by her desk. Lucy is a utilitarian minimalist and instead of girly trinkets, shallow 'live-laugh-love' signs or carefully arranged interior decoration, her living room contains a desk full of computer equipment, her nerd throne of a computer chair and a sofa.

"Doing alright. I'm getting some contracts from indie dreamers here and there," Lucy replies then spins her chair to face the monitor and starts typing at a speed not many mortals I've seen achieve.

The room is warm, uncomfortably so, even though the air conditioning box embedded in the window frame runs at max capacity and one of those huge industrial fans circulates air inside. They can barely keep up with the multiple servers, storage arrays and whatever other equipment she uses for mastering ramas.

"Cool... cool," I say standing there as she continues typing. After a couple minutes it's like she forgot I'm here. She could offer me a drink or ask me to have a seat. I don't want to stay here too late so I take the initiative and ask "well, what's this cool stuff you were going to show me."

She turns to look at me and says "oh yeah. Hold on." Then she continues typing. I see she's bringing up an encrypted directory then enters a password that seems to be 50 characters long. The contents of the encrypted directory expand in a browser window and Lucy stands and motions for me to sit in her nerd throne. "Check it out," she says.

From standing there I have no idea what I'm looking at so I nod, sit down and scroll down the contents of the directory. There are custom firmware files for some kind of diorama device, then I see a folder full of configuration files. I open one of them and start getting a slight idea of what these files are for.

"Is this firmware for operating a makeshift dreamcatcher?"

"Not only that," she says and I turn and look up to see her usual plain emotionless self, voice spiced up with a slight hint of arrogance. "I reverse engineered a legit neural catch driver and compiled mimic source code with directives that encode a random catcher ID in each rama frame at runtime."

I'm surprised by what I'm hearing. Sweet, nice girl Lucy. Who would have thought? Some of my shittyness probably rubbed off on her.

"But that would make any ramas caught with a device running these drivers completely anonymous. Untraceable," I say.

"Yeah," she nods.

"And also, very, very illegal," I clarify my point.

"Yeah."

"I mean, don't get me wrong Lucy, I'm impressed by the technical achievement. Respect where respect is due but someone finds this in your computer and you'll go to jail for a few years."

"Wasn't this what you wanted?" she says now mumbling in apparent distress. I've always wondered just how far in the spectrum she is. I never asked. Too embarrassing of a question.

"Well, yeah," I say trying to remember if my exact wording was to wish for software usually used by sex traffickers and anonymous dreamers who distribute illegal ramas all over the darkweb. "It would be cool to catch high quality ramas without paying the obscene licensing fees that professional equipment requires but damn."

"Oh," she says then approaches and I stand up to get out of her way. She sits back in her throne and types some more. "Well, I also got Chad's latest rama. It was just mastered yesterday."

"Not a fan."

"I copied the firmware in that flash drive," she says and motions with her head to the left side of her desk without taking her eyes off the screen.

I grab the flash drive. It's one of those fancy military grade models with built-in hardware encryption and self-destruct innards in case an attacker tries to disassemble to extract the NAND chips. Lucy continues to do whatever it is she's doing on her computer and I sit down in her sofa, behind her. Not only did she spend the time to do the hack but also the money for the drive.

"So why do all this?" I ask.

She turns away from the screen and looks at me then says "you're hardware, I'm software, remember? We're going to make and publish our own ramas and cash in the craze before it dies down."

I chuckle and shake my head. "You still remember? That

was pillow talk. What kind of rama can I make that attracts viewers and is not something illegal like those in the darkweb or near impossible to make like the sex vacations of Chad Mars that take millions of dollars to produce?"

Lucy rolls her eyes in that cute way of hers. I look at the military grade encrypted flash drive and ask myself if I'm creative enough to put something out there that millions of people would like. Who'd be the dreamer anyway?

"How's things at Dreamax?" she asks, breaking the silence but still keeping her attention on her computer screen.

"They announced downsizing today. Some people were already let go."

"Did you?"

"Nah, I still have a little leverage. I'm not as easily replaceable as Linda from HR would like."

She giggles for a couple seconds. I haven't seen her smile once since I walked in and now that she does, I can't see her face. "Linda from HR," she says. "That's funny, the way you say it."

"ToBogan was there today for a catch."

"Really? What kind of dangerous beast did he go bothering this time?"

"I don't know, the rama hasn't made it out of the catch shop."

"That's something you could dream about," she says, turning her chair. "You could explore abandoned buildings or factories. Or the deserted port of San Pedro in the middle of the night. We add ghosts in post or something. People like that kind of urban adventuring."

"Yeah and then my balls melt off from radiation. I'll pass."

Giving up, Lucy shrugs and goes back to her computer. She's probably spent the equivalent of a new car loan in all that equipment. Four 8k monitors, a main workstation, a storage array and a pretty beefy second workstation dedicated only to rama rendering. In her multitasking frenzy, I see her open a web browser and go to CNN, then she drags a news feed window to a side monitor I can see. President Trump is giving a speech while a sliding breaking news bar on the bottom contradicts every word she says.

"You pay too much attention to that crap," I say.

"I like to be informed before I cast a vote. Besides, it's entertaining," she says, pointing at the screen. "Now that the right hacked the identity politics the left first weaponized, there is very little the libs can say to discredit a female right-wing president."

"I don't know, I don't care," I say, pocketing the flash drive. "The way I see it, whoever is in power will fuck with whoever is not. Best thing we can do is try to gain a little bit of power ourselves so we don't get fucked with as easily."

Lucy doesn't have a rebuttal and continues typing. I guess she still remembers the hours-long debates on politics we used to engage in. The way I remember, they were smart exchanges I just couldn't get from the average mental slave, God forbid they got offended by me openly voicing unpopular opinions. Sometimes, if I was lucky, they would devolve into long sessions of angry sex but otherwise we'd mostly just walk away from each other in frustration. Politics and relationships just don't mix.

"Well, I've got to get going," I say, standing up. "Don't want to walk around your neighborhood past 8."

"Cool, good seeing you," she says, never letting her attention wander away from her workstation.

I show myself to the exit and close the door behind me. It would seem the hip hop army gave up and now the narco-corridos reign supreme, louder than before. A baby cries loudly somewhere in the distance. Who in their right mind would want to bring a kid to this shithole of a world?

The drive home is uneventful. A drunk homeless dude is passed out by the carport but I honk at him and eventually he drags himself out of the way, shouting what I think are obscenities in some language I can't understand.

It was good going out for a drive for once. I should go on a road trip. San Francisco or Vegas. Maybe bring Lucy along to catch up. Not sure how long she can stay away from her computers though.

My apartment is just the way I left it. Hasn't been tidied up for weeks. With no one to visit, there is little incentive for spending a couple hours doing so. I sit down in my own nerd throne and fire up the computer. While it boots up, I pull up the military grade flash drive with the scary illegal compiled binaries. Without much use for it, I just toss it in the pile with the others. Maybe I'll mess with it some other time. Right now, I must lurk. I must shitpost and debate TorChan armchair scholars. Got to get my daily dose of dopamine somehow.

4

Doing More With Less

It's been two weeks since our fearless leader and CEO Audrey Reynolds announced the 'strategic scale down'. Some people have already been let go while others watch the clock tick as the date of their official departure draws near. Must be horrifying, to invest your whole life and career to a niche industry. Me? I couldn't care less. All companies need IT in one way or another, but where do you even go when you're a Social Media Influencer Marketing Consultant? Or a Diorama Dreamcatcher Specialist? Yep, Scott was one of the first to get axed. Too bad, I liked the guy. Just another mind-slave in the herd, of course, but he'd show me cool stuff about dreamcatchers and all that.

Maybe the skillsets are transferable to other industries. But then, what do you do if you have a Master's Degree in Corporate Diversity or Chicano Studies or Women's Studies or whatever other useless stamped piece of paper given to you by a diploma mill and paid for by daddy's trust fund?

Where do you go if your job title is Social Media Diversity Awareness Officer? Or any other of those bogus jobs the company fills just to be able to say we're 'socially conscious'? It's good to have those on the payroll in case a Twitter 'influencer' bitches that your latest rama character is not a black gay disabled undocumented trans woman I guess. Can't have artistic license anymore. Must adhere to strict social justice guidelines in any content you create. Thanks, social justice warriors for killing the arts, among other things. No wonder people flocked to dioramas when the open source technology first emerged.

It's a quiet day on the second floor of Dreamax, a subsidiary of Tarios Group. I stand up to look around the open office from my cubicle. I can almost imagine a tumbleweed rolling by. With all the employee layoffs, there is not much need for people in the support money sinks around here. Rich was one of the first casualties. I hope he's having fun playing Minecraft wherever he is. Mary from HR is gone and now Linda from HR is all by herself. The Finance people are still untouched. They'll probably be the last to be shown the door, should the company tank for good.

The phone rings and I see Steve Kowalski's name in the caller ID. Senior Manager of Information Systems is his title. My boss' office is behind my cubicle and he couldn't just walk by if he needed something. I pick up the handset and greet the boss man.

"Hey Steve, what's up?"

"Ted when you got a minute, please come to my office," he says.

"Will do."

We hang up and I continue messing with the rama render engines for a few minutes. Yes, will be a while before I get a minute, Steve, you'll just have to wait for me. As I dick around with completely non-urgent work that could be placed on hold while I talk to him, it comes to me he's probably about to lay me off. I did update and post my resume online two weeks ago and I have 6 months' salary savings so I don't even care. Recruiters are already bugging me with potential leads. It's been a few minutes and I stand up to go to the restroom. Should be good enough to show the boss he doesn't get to say 'jump' and I ask 'how high?'

I come back from the gender-neutral restroom and knock on the open door to Steve's office.

"Ted, come in," he says with a smile. "Take a seat, please."

I make a concerned face. I hope I'm not overdoing it but it's funny to see his reaction when he thinks I'm terrified of being laid off. Probably too much. I feel bad about it and stop being a dick. Steve is a cool guy, probably the best guy I've ever worked for. Gives me a couple goals to achieve for the week and goes away to let me do my thing. The complete opposite of a micro manager. How would I call that? A macro manager? Whatever the official definition I hope the next boss is not the micro type.

"How's your day going?" Steve asks. "And how about those projects you're working on?"

"Well, you know, I'm making progress. Should have deliverables by their respective deadlines."

"Good, good," he says in that way people do when they ask something to make small talk but don't really care about your answer. "You let me know if you have any blockers for those deliverables and I'll take care of them."

"We're a team, boss," I say with a smile. Steve beams with happiness. He loves it when I call him 'boss' to his face. He talks about future deliverables. I guess I'm not being shown the door after all.

"Well, just to get it out of the way, you're not going to be let go," he says. Of course not. Who would do the actual work around here? "But we will see some new budget constraints. We'll need to go over each project you're working on. You know, the people upstairs want me to justify every dollar we're spending. You know how it is."

I nod and scoff then say "I know. Executives, am I right?"

"Yeah no kidding," Scott says and puts his elbows on the desk, hands clenched together near his chin. Oh shit, serious boss mode engaged. "The bad news is, after we're done talking, I'm going to pull Mia and Eric in here and sadly, I'm going to have to let them go."

Sucks for them. "They'll be alright. They're both good help desk technicians."

"Yep, it'll be just the two of us buddy."

Aww shit. Oh fuck. Does he mean what I think he means?

"We're going to have to do more with less," he says. "Since most of your projects are not critical to company revenue, we're going to put them on hold. Then you'll need to pick up the user-level tickets as you make progress on those projects we determine to be critical."

Oh god no. Don't make me deal with fucking PDF reader. "Huh," I mumble. Must make it look like I consider myself lucky to stay. "What percentage of my time you think I should spend on user-level support?"

"It would be hard to have an exact figure," my boss says as he reclines back on his chair in apparent relief. Probably expected me to bitch and moan. "I'd say prioritize trouble tickets and when there are none, work on long-term projects."

When there are no tickets? Is he joking? There are always tickets. Hundreds of them. The average office worker couldn't install PDF reader to save their life. For some reason in this day and age, basic computer literacy is not a skill required to get a job in a company that deals primarily in entertainment technology. Good for me, I suppose. Job security is always guaranteed.

"I understand," I say with a smile and a nod. "We'll do more with less."

"Excellent," Scott says. He always says 'excellent' to signal the end of a conversation for some reason. Guy thinks it makes him look clever. "Now if you'll excuse me, I have to give the bad news to Mia and Eric."

"Sure thing, boss. You know where to find me if you need anything."

Scott nods, pleased, and I walk out of his office. I haven't even reached my desk and I'm already pulling my phone out to check on the job hunt app. Six emails from recruiters. Hopefully I'll be out of this crumbling shithole by next week. I wonder if I should have overreacted and feigned outrage. Would have been funny to see Scott's reaction to me walking out. I've never done that dramatic exit kind of thing some people do.

I take a quick detour to the lunch room and get a mineral water from the vending machine. Even the break room is quiet. I'd usually find people engaged in half-hour long conversations that made me wonder just how useless and expendable their job is when they can walk away from their desk for an hour without anyone noticing. Unsurprisingly, it seems they were the first to go.

Back at my desk. Checking my emails. Checking the trouble tickets queue. I was working trouble tickets 10 years ago. I did my time in the trenches. I really don't want to go back to installing PDF reader. I open the job hunt app on my phone and message a couple of recruiters inquiring about jobs that look interesting. One of them for maintaining a supercomputer array at a USC research facility where they mess with gene sequencing. The other is to build a startup online presence from scratch. I'm surprised by how low the salaries are. I'm pretty sure I could handle either one but it would cost a considerable chunk of my current paycheck to leave Dreamax. I scroll down the list of job openings. Shitty salaries all over. The economy is just FUBAR. I realize I'm trapped here. I'm stuck installing PDF reader.

Fuck me.

5

Involuntary Requisition

Another week goes by. Another day working ten hours, dealing with computer illiterate people who get sassy when you explain how they fucked their own computer up and it's my job to clean up after them. Job hunt has not improved. I am now looking out of state. Maybe I land at Silicon Ranch up there in Montana.

I'm done for the day. I'm back home, my sanctuary of solitude, shitposting on TorChan. Maybe I should take a sabbatical like the hippies and trust fund babies do. Yeah, I could just quit the shitty job and maybe travel. It amazes me how mind bogglingly bored I am that I should even consider traveling. I never understood, the resources some people spend on packing up, flying to some place a thousand miles away, just so they can post selfies on Instagram and make their cardboard friends jealous. I suppose traveling used to mean something. One could go somewhere far away from one's country and learn from how people do things outside of what we consider normal. Nowadays it's just an expensive, dumbed down activity for vapid people to one up each other on social media. Just like everything else.

There's that little voice again. That annoying little reminder in the back of my mind that I should be doing something productive with my life. That horrifying feeling that one day I'll be experiencing my last few seconds in this world and all I'll remember will be my long TorChan shitposting sessions. I recline back on my computer chair and put my feet up on the desk then take a sip from the bottle. This time it's a weird Japanese pale ale. Nothing but moon runes on the label. Sure, there's a little translated nutritional facts label but other than that, the factory label could state it was made from dog shit for all I know. Even if that was the case, it would be great tasting dog shit.

I take a short break from shitposting. No doubt I'll find another thread to troll. My eyes focus on the pile of unused flash drives on a shelf. They're all in this little cereal bowl I put there to throw loose change in. At some point I started filling it up with flash drives too. And on top of the little pile, that super-secure military grade drive that Lucy gave me catches my attention. So small but filled with binaries that could get me sent to jail. Then again, most darkweb ramas are recorded with similar software. There are probably hundreds of thousands if not millions of ramas out there. No law enforcement agency would have the resources to track them all down. Even if they did, I'd be able to encode a rama so it's untraceable.

So mindbogglingly bored I am that I stand up, walk the few steps between my nerd throne and the shelf to grab the flash drive. I sit back down and fire up a secure sandbox then plug the thing to my workstation. Not only did she reverse engineer proprietary software and recompiled new binaries from scratch, she even wrote some documentation on how to install properly.

I look around my apartment. It's a disgusting pigsty as usual. No one ever visits so why should I slave over keeping it shiny? It's a disgusting mess but it's my mess. And amongst the mess, I keep some discarded dreamcatcher parts. Some I lifted from Dreamax, others I bought online. The little voice in my head yelling to stop wasting my life got me to enroll in a learning annex class for entrepreneurs looking to open their own rama-related business some years ago. It became a hobby to learn how to take them apart and see how they work but I never actually caught any ramas out of my own head.

There are enough parts to get a rough prototype going, except for one last crucial component too expensive for a hobbyist. The neural scanner. A set of interconnected sensors that scan a dreamer's memory centers in the brain so the target memory can be found and copied to encoder equipment. They're tiny but made out of very specialized parts. A used unit can be had for about $100k. Regardless, even with the missing component I can still install Lucy's custom firmware and boot the thing up. The end result is a device that resembles a bicycle helmet and feels heavier than it looks. As the thing boots up, connected to my computer, I can see diagnostics text scrolling rapidly on my screen. Then an error stops the whole process.

Catastrophic Error: Neural Scanner Missing

Maybe I should be training for some new hot skill that would land me a job faster. I wonder why I'm still wasting my time with this thing. I unplug it from the computer and put it aside. My dopamine addiction calls for me and so I open my secure web browser and make for TorChan.

*

The next day I take a walk to the catch shop, mineral water in hand. I look around the once busy room now empty, save for the new man in charge who sees me and approaches to say hi.

"Ted, how you doing?"

"Living the dream, Ben. Living the dream," I reply.

With Scott gone, the man in charge is a dude named Ben. Nothing against him but he was Scott's intern last year. Scott went to engineering school and spent years in the field. The guy knows everything there is to know about any professional equipment used in the studio diorama business. Too bad an MBA upstairs decided it would be cheaper to have an intern take over his job. Of course, anything breaks that Ben can't handle and he calls a contractor who charges triple of what Scott was making to drive onsite the next day and fix it. Just another genius MBA decision, validated by a stamped piece of paper from a pricey diploma mill.

"Damn, you don't have any dreamers for intake today?" I ask, looking around the deserted shop.

"Not until Thursday, my dude," he replies. What an odd expression 'my dude' is. As if the youngsters don't understand the homoerotic implications. Or maybe they do and it's used ironically just like every god damn thing with their generation.

"Huh," I mumble. There are 4 intake chairs and each one has a neural scanner inside its headrest.

"I hear ToBogan is still in LA," he adds, as he walks back to one of the chairs workstation. "But I think his latest rama is already in post."

"Really? What is it about this time?"

"He went mapping some undiscovered bends of the Naracoorte Caves. I've dreamed some raw clips, since I'm also helping with post."

"Man of many talents," I say with a smile. Ben seems pleased and returns the gesture. Poor guy. Probably overworked in two departments, underpaid but still sticking around by the promise of a place in the booming studio rama industry. Old Hollywood practices with nowhere near the same money or perks.

The former intern continues doing whatever it is he's doing and I look up to the ceiling. There are 4 security cameras, each covering one another's blind spots. Makes sense, the catch shop houses a few million dollars' worth of equipment.

"What brings you down here anyway?" Ben asks from his workstation.

"Someone reported weak WiFi signal," I reply as I scan the ceiling. "Just looking for a wireless access point with a blinking amber light."

"Well, at least you're busy."

"Why? You're not?"

"Nah," says Ben. He stands up and leans against the edge of the catch chair, arms crossed. "Not much to do. The next catch is not for a couple weeks when Steph comes back with the Wimbledon experience in her head."

Stephanie? The name doesn't ring a bell. Probably one of the dozens of anonymous dreamers we employ when the focus of the rama is the experience and not the celebrity dreamer.

"No kidding," I say, looking down. "Maybe the leadership will sell the extra chairs. Do you even use them all at the same time?"

"That's an idea. We don't. In fact, this is the only one in use, at least until the budget increases and we get some projects greenlit."

Ben taps his hand on the chair he's leaning on. The third one from the left. The first one is not even powered on. No one would notice if a certain key part was removed from it.

"Hey, let's do lunch later," I say. "I want to hear everything you know about catching ramas."

He scoffs and shakes his head. "You're kidding right? You probably know more than me, I've only been here 2 weeks."

"Then it'll be an exchange of ideas," I say and turn around to get back to my desk. "Ping me at whatever time it is you usually eat."

"Yeah, will do."

Back at my desk, I look up the surveillance server. The Security guys are too lazy to maintain the thing so they usually just dump on me the task of calling the company that installed it whenever anything breaks. It used to piss me off to no end but now it might come in handy. These guys are supposed to be in charge of loss prevention but they don't seem to give a shit. They make it just too easy to social engineer my way in. I type the root password to the surveillance system and list the available cameras. Luckily, they're categorized by department so it takes a minute to bring up a view of the catch shop. Four cameras and only one covers the entrance and the leftmost catch chair.

I minimize the surveillance system window and go back to work the tickets. Someone doesn't know how to setup an email signature. Another lost soul disabled his laptop touchpad and doesn't know how to make it work again. These people grew up with smartphones and were babysat by tablets and they're still incapable of doing a web search that would take seconds. Job security for me I guess.

The morning drags on but eventually I get a chat message from Ben.

    From: Ben Alcivar
    Food when?

Ah, yes. Modern dumbed down text message English.

    From: Ben Alcivar
    Food when?
                        From Me:
                        You're going now?

From: Ben Alcivar
Yah hungry

From Me:
Sorry dude, I got
swamped with work. Can't
make it today.
Maybe some other time.

From: Ben Alcivar
It cool bruh ttyl

I bring back the surveillance system and I see Ben walk out of the shop. From another, unrelated computer, I start a network flood attack. Little by little, the network interface of the target camera gets overwhelmed with garbage traffic and the video feed suffers. Frames are skipped, video resolution grinds below SD. It doesn't take long for the poor thing to give out and the surveillance server marks the camera as 'needing maintenance.' A small pop-up in the corner of the window tells me the surveillance system vendor has been notified. I lock my computer and stand up.

When I get there, the catch shop is still empty. Not even a janitor around. As I walk in and make for the leftmost catch chair, I realize I've been humming the Mission Impossible theme. These chairs are made prioritizing dreamer comfort. It's like a sofa-padded dentist chair. The headrest looks like any other. I unzip it from the bottom and lift the leather and padding and there it is, in all it's $100,000 glory, the neural scanner. I giggle like a schoolgirl when I pull it out and the daisy-chained sensors encased in protective plastic spheres remind me of anal beads. It's small enough that it fits in one of my cargo shorts pockets. The spy theme playing in my head intensifies.

I walk back to my desk but first make a quick detour to the lunch room to get a mineral water, which will be my alibi

41

in case anyone in Security with half a brain sees me going in the direction of the catch shop in the other cameras. Not too slow but not too fast either. Nonetheless I still hyperventilate a little. Fuck, I'm so out of shape. I sit down at my workstation and lightly pad my pocket just to confirm the sophisticated piece of equipment is still there. The computer is just the way I left it. I login and stop the network attack then do a secure wipe of the software I used for it. In the surveillance panel, I see the video feed slowly returning. The phone rings. I see Ed Kelly in the caller ID. Manager of Facilities Security and Loss Prevention is his title.

"Hey Ed, what's up?"

"Not much, Ted, the usual," he replies. He sounds tired. Probably worked the night shift and now my superspy antics are keeping him from going home. "Hey, I see you logged in to the surveillance system. Did anything break?"

"Yeah, but nothing related to your stuff," I say with that high-pitched effeminate tone of voice that instantly lowers his defenses. I've never had any non-work-related conversations with the guy but I can tell he's a walking concoction of steroids and testosterone. Very muscular. A regular to the gym. Most likely looks down on fatties like me as if we're shameful wastes of masculinity. All I have to do is pretend his muscle mass intimidates me so he'd never think of me as a threat. "I'm very sorry but one of our servers' network interface malfunctioned and was sending garbage data to one of your cameras but I found it and…"

"Yeah yeah, whatever technical stuff you did, is it fixed?" Ed interrupts to double down his assertion of alpha-ness over me, a lowly omega in the micro society of Dreamax.

"Yeah, it's all good now. I was just checking the camera didn't get damaged by the…" I try to come up with a bullshit technical-sounding term that will go over his head and luckily will forget when he writes his incident report. "… TCP SYN flux flooding the ethernet channel…"

"Okay, whatever. Be a good pal and call the vendor to tell them there is no need to stop by, will you?"

"Sure thing, Ed. Anything I can do to help."

"Sounds good. I won't even write a report since you fixed it right away."

"Thanks, Ed. I'm happy to help," I say but Ed hangs up before I finish the sentence. It boggles the mind these guys who are supposed to safeguard the assets of a multi-million dollar company are not trained to smell social engineering.

I smile and the last few notes of the Mission Impossible theme go through my mind as I tap the anal beads in my pocket.

6

The Business Partner

"What do you want?" is the first thing Lucy asks when the apartment door opens and her head pops out.

"I can't visit every now and then?" I reply innocently.

"Whatever," she says, turning around and leaving the door open for me to step in. "Text me or something first, I could have had a guy in here."

Yeah, sure. "My bad, I will next time."

I walk in Lucy's apartment and the warmth of her rendering computers hits me. There's a slight BO in the air and I realize she's just embarrassed she couldn't take a shower before I showed up unexpected. I take off my backpack and put it on the sofa then sit next to it. Lucy is already sitting down at her nerd throne to continue whatever she was working on.

"So how you've been?" I ask.

She mumbles something then takes a sip of diet cola.

"Well, I have a surprise for you."

Lucy immediately stops what she's doing and turns her nerd throne to face me, curiosity aroused. Oh yeah Lucy still loves surprises. There's even a hint of a smile in that face half-buried in messy short black hair.

"What is it?"

Without answering, I reach for my backpack, slowly unzip it then pull out an object she stares at confused.

"A bicycle helmet?" she asks disappointed. "I don't even own a bike."

Smiling, I stand up and approach to put it in her hands. "Take a closer look."

She looks at me cautiously like I just handed her a bomb then examines the thing. On close inspection, she seems to realize it's not a bike helmet, then she finds the cabling, battery and other electronic components I somehow managed to cram into the compact design.

"You built it!" she exclaims with a wide grin. It's nice to see her genuinely smile every now and then.

"Yep."

"Did my drivers work?" she asks then puts it on as if to test if it's comfortable to wear.

"It boots up but I haven't tried catching anything."

"Huh," Lucy mumbles, taking off the contraption.

"I took some liberties with the design," I explain. Lucy puts the protype dreamcatcher on her lap and listens attentively. "I figured if we're going to produce ramas, the dreamcatcher would need to be portable enough to bring to people I could persuade to sell me some raw catches. The catch process would also have to be much faster and cause less discomfort for the dreamer. I guess if I can make the catch as fast, painless and convenient as possible, I'd be able to get away with paying less."

"You have the whole business model figured out, don't you?" Lucy asks... sarcastically?

"Well yeah. The problem is, in order to make a dreamcatcher work faster and painlessly, the scan and copy process has to be more aggressive while at the same time messing with the brain's pain centers to mitigate the assault.

I don't know if anyone has tried that approach, or if it's safe."

Lucy returns her attention to the dreamcatcher and nods slightly. I can almost hear the gears turning inside her head. Back when we first met, she was a rama post-production engineer at Dreamax. It was in a random lunchtime conversation that we figured neither one of us wanted to be wage slaves for too long. The job was only a way to learn a skill that could be used outside to run our own business. Now that I think about it, that's probably what became the basis for our relationship. But for all our ambition and technical knowledge, we could never crack the code of what made someone like Chad Mars so insanely popular while thousands of other indie dreamers had small fanbases but never quite broke out of their niche to appeal to the masses.

When the open source code that'd drive diorama technology first emerged online, no one cared about it. It was just not a lot of fun to picture oneself alone in a room, with a headset on and fully disconnected from the world to dream the ramas of random people. No, people still wanted to go watch movies with friends. Entertainment was a social affair. It wasn't until Chad Mars opened a RamaHub account, with his already large following of creepy dudes dreaming his wet dream ramas of trips to countries with a questionable age of consent that the slaves at large paid attention to the technology. Suddenly sex tourism became socially acceptable. In a world where most people are living check to check, his mainstream dioramas of expensive vacations and exotic places attracted millions of slaves desperate to escape their miserable lives. And so, an already rich man who had it all became even richer.

"So now what?" Lucy asks, probably as excited as me at the possibility of making our business dreams come true. "We find someone who would agree to risk their lives to test it?"

"We could find a partner. A third person in the team," I explain my weak idea. "Someone to dream while we work the technology and business side of things."

"Oh, I know," she says. "We put up an ad on Craigslist. Diorama startup with no capital seeks partner willing to get their brain fried in exchange for the possibility of a few dollars in residuals." Oh, she's being sarcastic. "Borderline suicidal people preferred."

"Okay, okay I get it," I say with a smirk. "It's a shitty idea but I don't hear any from you."

No rebuttal. Lucy puts the dreamcatcher on her desk and reclines on her nerd throne, head tilted back. For a few minutes we both sit there in awkward silence, apparently trying our best to solve the problem of finding someone who'd let us a) fry their brain and b) dream dioramas for our profit.

Then it comes to me. An idea as brilliant as it is fucked up. No, even if I say it out loud, Lucy would never agree to such a depraved abuse of a fellow human being. Then again, no one would care regardless of the consequences. We built a god damn anonymous dreamcatcher. No one would be able to trace it back to us, should the worst happen. I look at Lucy, who, as if reading my mind, lifts her head from the nerd throne headrest and looks me in the eyes expectantly, ready to hear my brilliant plan.

"We catch a random rama off a homeless dude," I say bluntly. Why even try to sugarcoat it?

To my astonishment, Lucy nods with a wide grin as she says "fuck yeah."

*

It's almost 10 PM in Downtown LA. I exit the 101 at Temple, go south at Grand and continue the drive past Grand Park.

"Where are you going?" Lucy asks. "Huge tent city right here."

"Yeah, that's why it's not good for us," I reply. I know the neighborhood don't argue with me. "There are all kinds of non-profit offices around Grand Park and they're open 24-7."

"What do they do?"

"The usual, free food, free tents, free rama visors, free condoms, free HIV testing and whatever else our mentally ill populace might need to enable their permanent homeless lifestyle."

"Armchair sociology expert over here. So then what should be done to address the homeless problem? Please enlighten me."

I turn to see her and she smiles, knowing that's one of the many buttons she can push to annoy me. Politics.

"All other cities around LA have vagrancy laws, why not us? It just lets them bus their homeless here where they know no one will do anything about it."

"You didn't answer the question. Should we round them up in concentration camps? Maybe ship them out of state?"

"I don't know," I answer with a shrug. "Most of these people are too mentally gone to fit with society and we're not going to put them in old timey hellish sanatoriums either. I guess we'll just have to deal with the smell and go on with our lives. Doesn't deny the fact it's good business for the non-profits."

"There's a reason they're called 'non-profits' you know?"

"Yeah right. Somewhere, somehow, someone is making money from all this misery. It's the American way."

Lucy scoffs and turns to look out her window. Through our relationship, she was the voice of reason to counter my extreme cynicism but now she seems closer to my fucked-up worldview than she was when we broke up. Confirms my theory if you want to see the world the way it truly is, all you need is to let it sucker punch you a few times so you grow older and wiser.

We arrive close to our destination and I park a block away. Lucy looks around in confusion but I point south, where she finds the 24-7 activity of the Pershing Square tent city.

"Let me have that," I say and grab the dreamcatcher off her hands to put inside my backpack. I then exit the car and she follows.

"What's the plan then?" Lucy asks.

"I got a twenty with me, I figure that should be enough for the average druggie."

She nods in agreement and we walk down the block and cross the street to continue away from the car. The smell is almost unbearable this close. I turn left to take a look at the tent city built inside and on top the abandoned Pershing Square parking lot. The stink of excrement, urine and miscellaneous bodily odors waft in the air. One can only imagine how concentrated it is below in the three parking sublevels underneath. Who knows what happens there too. Police by law are not allowed to touch or even speak to a vagrant, God forbid they hurt their feelings. Smart entrepreneurs working in the lucrative prostitution, illegal drugs and human trafficking industries know all they have to do is surround their headquarters with a huge stinking mass of mentally ill people and they'll be shielded against police surveillance. Now that I think about it, probably not a great idea to walk around here this late at night.

"How about that one?" Lucy points at an obese woman in the distance who is away from the crowd, sitting in a park bench and moving her upper body rhythmically whilst speaking in tongues.

"I don't know, doesn't look like she can be talked to," I say as if verbally agreeing to a $20 exchange for a life-threatening rama capture would make the transaction any less morally or legally questionable.

Lucy shrugs and looks around. We continue down the outskirts of the tent city then cross the street, putting us two blocks away from the car. Most storefronts are boarded up. And to think just a few years ago they carried millions of dollars in diamonds and jewelry. A mentally disturbed dude screams in the distance and the scream is followed by the sound of a glass bottle shattering. This spooks Lucy, who now finally seems to realize it's not very safe around here. She grabs my arm and holds herself closer to me. It's nice, the feeling of human warmth.

At least it's cooled down but not so that I'd have to wear a jacket. Lucy, on the other hand is not shielded against exposure to the elements the way my fat rolls do for me so I feel a slight shiver in her hands. As I wonder just what hell are we looking for exactly, we walk past an alley. I stop immediately and Lucy looks at me, confused. I'm pretty sure I saw movement down there so we backtrack a little bit to confirm a few feet down the alley, someone is sitting by themselves behind an overflowed orange trash container. I don't hear gibberish or, dark as it is, see involuntary body movements. Maybe it's just a wino we can actually talk to.

I can see the homeless dude's leg from the sidewalk and I point there. Lucy nods in agreement and she follows me towards it. We get closer and from up close I can hear sounds. Grunts? We reach the other side of the trash container and find a man, who probably hasn't showered in years, pants down, vigorously masturbating in the open.

Lucy dry heaves and hurries back to the sidewalk. I stand there, frozen. One of those kinds of situations where the brain locks up, struggling to come up with an appropriate reaction for an extremely unlikely scenario. I keep looking down and the man enjoying himself looks up and we lock eyes for a few seconds. He licks his lips through a subtle smile and his hand starts moving faster. This is where I decide that's enough and follow Lucy away from this guy.

"Well, that happened," she says when I meet her on the sidewalk.

I shrug and say "it's the price of doing business I suppose."

"At least he seems not too far gone," she adds, looking away probably in embarrassment. "Best specimen we have found so far."

"So... we wait here until he's done?"

"Yeah. I mean how long could it take? How long does it take you?"

"Are you seriously asking how long it takes me to jerk off?" I ask, frankly offended at the blatant attempt to violate my privacy. But then I wonder what the median would be. So many factors usually go into determining how long or short it could go. Someone should gather statistical data on the subject. Maybe it could be a question in the next census.

She giggles and looks down, holding her arms around herself for warmth. I just stand there with my hands in my pockets. We silently agree to wait there awkwardly within earshot of the grunts and accelerated breathing of the nameless, homeless guy pleasuring himself.

"You ever miss us?" Fuck. Why do girls have to ask such cliché questions? Anything to mask the jerking off sounds ten feet away from us, I guess.

"Sometimes," I say, still looking away at nothing in particular. Feels like I should follow that up with something deep but nothing comes to mind.

"I mean, just when things were getting serious, one day you decide to just walk away," she says. We've kept in touch but never talked about it until now. Now that I think about it, she probably has things to say. Odd choice of setting to do so. "And your 'it's not you, it's me' bullshit didn't explain much."

I sigh and look down at my feet. Such a cliché reason to break up too. She got me there.

"I don't know," I lie. I do know. But some things are hard to put in words. "Been alone my whole life, something unsettling about one day just letting someone in."

Lucy scoffs and rolls her eyes then says "right. More bullshit."

"I'm sorry, I don't know what else to say."

"Huh," she mumbles and our eyes meet. "You choose solitude over the 'unsettling' feeling of not being alone anymore? I just don't get it."

"Yeah, you don't," I say. In the distance, the breathing speeds up. Sounds like he's almost done. God damn, how long can an orgasm last? "Look, I'm sure there's a swarm of nerds out there who would fight over you. You're a woman, all you have to do is not be morbidly obese and some guy somewhere will ask you out."

"Now you're the one who doesn't get it," she says. "People don't just push each other out of their lives like that, even I know that."

"Well, that's who I am. Fucked up to the core."

Just when the situation couldn't be any more uncomfortable, I hear our friend in the back take a couple deep breaths, signaling he is done. I'm glad our emotional heart-to-heart is over but now we should get back to business.

"Look, we'll talk about it later," I say. Lucy gives me a disapproving look with those big brown eyes that see through me, piercing through my defenses, reading me like an open book when I put so much energy into keeping it closed to others. I despise that feeling, that I would enable any one person to have this much power over me. The power to control my emotions, to dictate if I should be happy or not. Fuck that.

I sigh, doing my best to push the anger out of me and walk towards our potential business partner. Lucy follows closely behind. Bracing for another shocking sight, I reach the other side of the trash container and my eyes get used to the darkness to find our friend laying on his back with a blissful expression on his face, flaccid penis in his hand, semen all over the place. I see a filthy blanket on the side and reach for it to cover him.

"Is it safe?" Lucy asks. I turn and see her covering her face but still seeing through the gaps between her fingers.

"Yeah," I say and motion with my head to come closer.

Our potential business partner reeks of sour body odor and alcohol. He looks like an older gentleman, long grey hair and a longer grey beard. There are several discarded cans and bottles next to him and what looks like a begging sign with the typical 'god bless' scribbled on it. His eyes stare into nothing, maybe still enjoying the post-orgasm dopamine rush.

I squat to be closer to his eye level and say "good evening to you, sir."

The homeless man seems to react and his eyes slowly move away from the void to focus on mine. He grunts, mouth agape. Christ, the smell. I figure he won't be the talkative type and pull the $20 bill out of my pocket and hold it up, making sure the light from the street makes it visible enough. Suddenly, the life comes back to him and he reaches for the bill as he stares at it.

"Wait, wait, wait, hold on," I say, extending my hand away from his grasp. "I have a business proposition for you."

"What?" he asks with a heavily slurred voice.

"We would like to contract certain services from you, in exchange for this," I clarify.

"S-services? What?"

I stand up and pull the prototype dreamcatcher out of my backpack to show it to him and continue to explain my value proposition. "I would like you to wear this helmet for about ten minutes. We'll pay for your time, of course."

There's a glimpse of understanding in his eyes and he nods rapidly, I guess imagining all the bootleg booze he could buy with that twenty. I figure that's good enough for the courts if it comes to it. Consent was requested of the potentially offended party and the potentially offended party gave consent. Damn, in another life, I probably would have been a lawyer.

Our no longer potential business partner seems excited to join our business venture and so without prolonging the process any more, I put the 'catcher on him and power it on.

"Half hour, no more," I remind our friend and he nods. Good.

"Well, that was easy," Lucy points out.

"Yeah," I say and pull my laptop out of the backpack. I bring it out of sleep and establish a wireless connection with the dreamcatcher. On the controller software, I see normal operation and the device has detected a suitable brain to run a catch from. I click a couple buttons and the process starts.

"Woah," says Lucy when the progress bar moves five points or so every second.

"Yep," I say, smug smile and all. "Express diorama catching."

There's no need to even ask our business partner to focus on a memory to give us an entry point. The prototype dreamcatcher finds one and locks in, reporting a diorama is being caught within seconds. I look at him and he continues to lie there looking at me then at Lucy and then back and forth every few seconds.

Something's wrong. The diorama catch progress bar stops at 43%. I look back at the homeless guy and his eyes are closed. He seems to have lost consciousness. Fuck me.

"Could you hold this for a moment?" I ask Lucy as I hand her the laptop. I squat again, cursing having to do so because of how much it hurts my knees. "Hey dude, you okay?" I ask, tapping his cheek a little.

Out of nowhere, our business partner snaps out of it and grabs my shirt. Startled, I try to pull back but he's holding on to me with superhuman strength and I stumble, falling on my back with this dude now on top of me, growling, and I see pure rage in his eyes. I look up at Lucy and she's freaking out while I lie there on a puddle of what reeks of sewage.

"It's moving along," says Lucy, as if this would comfort me in my current situation.

"Okay," I say, nodding, while keeping the feral wino from biting my face off. It dawns on me he's not in pain or else he would have simply reached for the dreamcatcher to take it off his head. No, he's intensely focused on me, angry. Whatever the prototype is catching, he's reliving that memory and it's not a pleasant one.

"Seventy percent," Lucy updates me.

He's an old man but still somehow musters the strength to overpower me. I decide I'm about done putting up with it and knee him, I think in the stomach. Maybe in the balls. Who cares? It's enough to get him off me. Our soon to be former business partner now lies on his back. Luckily his head didn't land in the puddle so the 'catcher is still dry.

"Done," Lucy announces then approaches, apparently to help me get up but then the smell hits her and she recoils as she goes "eww."

It's fine, I manage to get myself off my ass. God damn why does it have to stink so much? I try to shake the disgusting water off my clothes then ask Lucy "we have a good catch at least?"

"Yeah," she replies with a smile and shows me the laptop screen where my exact question is answered.

I nod then kneel down to remove the dreamcatcher off the wino. At least the catch didn't kill him. He's just lying there, sleeping. I'm surprised the prototype didn't get shattered by all the commotion. I guess it's a testament to my excellent craftmanship. Some unknown goop from the wino's hair is stuck to the insides of it though. I'll need to replace the whole casing. No way I'm washing that filth off. My backpack is a few steps away. I walk there and grab it. As I put the prototype inside I realize the backpack will be ruined. Fuck, my car will be ruined when I get in. Hopefully, the detailers at the corner car wash can remove whatever odors remain after I get home and shower. I might have to replace the seats.

"You better hold on to the laptop," I tell Lucy who nods in agreement and closes it. "I guess we're done here."

*

Lucy holds the door for me to get into her apartment but keeps her distance, not in the least hiding how disgusted she is.

"Wait!" she exclaims then runs to her room and pulls out a discarded cardboard box. Probably one of her servers came in it. She flattens and places it on her carpet and points so I stand there.

"So I'm just going to stand here?"

"Ugh," she grunts in disgust. "Hand me the thing."

I take my backpack off, open it and place the dreamcatcher prototype on her hands. She carefully grabs it from the edges as to not touch the hair goop from the wino.

"Ugh… eww," she continues complaining in disgust. For a fleeting moment, I imagine jumping and giving her a bear hug just so she can be as stinky as I am but decide against it. Probably not the right thing to do to your ex. Especially not after that chat we had not too long ago.

She sits in her nerd throne and plugs the dreamcatcher to a computer then, without even looking at me says "go, take a shower. Just don't make a mess of my bathroom."

"And what am I going to wear after?" I ask looking down at myself.

"Well…" she says. "You forgot one of your bathrobes. Found it under the bed a while ago."

"And you kept it?" I ask with a smirk. "That's kind of creepy."

She turns, ready for a rebuttal, but instead just goes "ugh," as she rolls her eyes and turns back to continue typing on her keyboard. "Just go, you're stinking up my place."

Might as well, although I'm going to have to shower again when I get home, since the car seat is soaked with shit water. Oh well, I'm a guest, might as well respect the wishes of my host. I wipe my sneakers on the carboard box to make sure I won't leave a trail of shit water behind me then make for her bathroom. A strong scent of cherries hits me when I open the door. Like she had a dozen air fresheners running at max power in here or something. In contrast, my bathroom only has one of two possible smells: neutral and shit. Lucy still keeps spare plastic bags in a drawer for the waste basket so I pull one out. Carefully, I remove my wallet, keychain and my -luckily waterproof- smartphone and put them inside the bag. I pull another out of the drawer and proceed to remove my shit-soaked clothes and put them in it. Her tub has one of those detachable showerheads I always wondered if she used for masturbatory purposes.

I don't take too long in here as she might think I'm jerking off or something. I get out and dry myself with her towel. I'll need to remember buying her a replacement. While I was showering, she placed the aforementioned bathrobe on her bed so I grab and put it on. She even washed it. Smells like a fresh summer breeze, or at least the scent fresh summer breezes are supposed to have according to laundry detergent manufacturers. No sandals. Fuck I hate walking around barefoot.

Back in her living room, I walk past Lucy who doesn't acknowledge my presence and continues typing. I sit in her couch and wonder just how late it is. It doesn't seem like she'll react so I ask "so, do we have a diorama?"

"Yeah, but it's strange," she replies. Shit, I hope it's usable.

"Strange how?"

"Here," she says and points to something on her monitor. I stand up to get close and see a graph with a bunch of lines plotted on it.

"What's strange about a standard brainwave graph?"

"Hold on," says Lucy then type something. The graph reloads but I notice the lines are plotted at different values.

"That doesn't make any sense. Now we're now looking at a completely different diorama."

"No, it's the same one," she says and clicks a button that redraws the graph with a new set of values.

"Fuck," I say and cross my arms. "It's corrupted then."

"I don't think so. Integrity checks run normally," she says turns to look at me. "You want to stop by tomorrow after work to check it out?"

"Huh?" I respond abruptly. "After all I went through? I want to dream it now. I'll just send an email to the boss man and tell him I came down with the flu. I mean unless you want to go to bed."

"No, I want to find out too."

"Alright then, is it ready?"

"Yeah," she says and stands up. From underneath her desk, she pulls an immersion visor. Oneiros brand. I like those, they're high quality. She runs its long cable across the living room and places it on the sofa then motions for me to lie down.

"I'm naked under this robe, don't molest me while I'm out," I say. She gives me a 'bitch, please' look I shrug off then sit in the couch and lie with my head near the visor. She puts it on carefully. All lights go out.

"Have fun," I hear her say over the earphones then the visor comes to life and reality warps in front of my eyes.

7

Full Catch Diorama

I open my eyes and find myself standing next to a car, parked on the driveway of an upper-class-looking house in what looks like an upper-class neighborhood. It's late at night, chilly. There's something strange about the overall scene. As if I was watching a video with its brightness drastically dimmed down. Shadows look pitch black. Probably a byproduct of dreaming the diorama of a chronic alcoholic. Looks like our good ol' wino friend did well for himself at some point of his life. I'm just relieved the diorama we caught was not corrupted. I guess it was totally worth it to swim in shit water for a couple of minutes.

My wino friend looks down and from his perspective, I see him pull his keys out of a pocket and walks towards the front door. Just like any other diorama, I am reliving this scene from one of his memories as if I was him. It seems I am wearing a suit and tie and holding a briefcase with my left hand. I approach the door, unlock it and step in. It's curious how my eyes don't even adapt to the darkness but somehow, I know where to go and find a switch. When the lights come on, it surprises me how expensive everything looks inside. I kind of feel sorry for our wino business partner, it seems the poor guy fell down from a stable life pretty hard. That's alcohol for you. I feel tired. Exhausted. Like I just came back from hell at wherever it is this anonymous wino dude used to work. Some relief comes from loosening my necktie.

All I want is to do is get to my bed and sleep forever. There are no clocks I can see. No idea what time it is. I'm glad the dreamcatcher works but this rama won't attract many viewers. Fuck me, I'm going to have to find a way to pay legitimate dreamers. Anyway, I climb the staircase and open the door to my room. I hear noise inside. I turn the lights on and I see my wife in bed with my brother. They're... naked? I clutch the briefcase handle as hard as I can but it feels different somehow. I lift my left hand and find an unsheathed army knife instead. My wife is crying apologies that go to deaf ears. My brother is freaking out. He sits there, on the bed, butt naked, trying to explain the betrayal but I hear nothing. Their voices sound distant, distorted. I don't want to hear excuses. I feel rage. I feel pain. Exhaustion goes away in an instant and I feel an adrenaline rush overriding rational thought.

Jesus Christ, his brother fucked his wife. I want to feel sorry for the guy but instead all I can sense is fury and I agree with him. I'm furious myself. Fuck this asshole and fuck this bitch. They're going to die. I punch my brother as hard as I can and he falls to the floor face down. An opening. I grab the knife with both hands and stab the motherfucker as hard as I can. Steel cuts through skin then deep inside his flesh. He screams in agony and coughs blood. This is not enough. More. He must die. This fucker. This dog. This fucking animal that shares my blood. Tears run down my face, slightly blurring my sight.

In a far distance, my wife cries, as I stab my brother over and over again, hands sticky with his blood. He is moving no more.

She cries hysterically. My wife. The woman I loved. The woman I still love. The diorama immersion breaks my heart. I feel this man's fury. I feel his pain as if mine. He's been betrayed in unspeakable ways and now he's ruined his life. This isn't fair.

I gave her everything. I sacrificed much for her. I was always faithful despite plenty of opportunities to not be. I put up with her fucking mother and her constant sarcasm. I got myself in debt for the rest of my life to provide the house she wanted in the neighborhood she wanted. And the cars and the clothes and the jewelry and the expensive vacations. She was my high school sweetheart. The only woman I've ever been with. I thought we had something that transcended reason. I thought we had a connection.

But she fucked my brother.

I look away from my blood-soaked hands. There she is, cornered against the wall. Naked. Covered in sweat and the saliva and the cum of my brother. This fucking whore. She pleads for her life but at this point, there is no reasoning with me. Common sense and self-preservation get pushed way in the back of my head and only rage prevails. I walk to her and swiftly grab her by the neck with my free hand. Streaks of coagulating blood stain her face and her neck. There. She is now covered in all of my brother's bodily fluids. Wait, what about piss? The stupidity of such a thought crossing my mind at this moment makes me laugh. And I laugh loudly. Maniacally. She's in shock. She is crying no more. She is begging no more. She just stares at me like some stupid beast, unable to comprehend the world around it.

With a swift motion, I thrust the knife into her. I pull it out. I thrust again. Then again, and again. Yeah, her lower abdomen. Her cunt. Her thighs. She looks at me, silently, eyes wide open, then a whimper escapes and her eyes go white. She passes out then dies while I still hold her.

The knife drops to the floor, followed by the mass of flesh that was my wife just moments ago. I sit on the edge of the bed and stare at her. I admire her nude blood-covered beauty. There's no going back from this but this man somehow still avoided jail and made it into the Pershing Square tent city. I cry but I can't wipe my tears. Hands covered in blood and all. Why did she make me do this? Why?

There are no answers. In the distance, I hear police sirens approach. The neighbors probably heard the commotion and the screaming. This is the most raw, intense diorama I've ever been immersed into. We're going to be rich. It's short but intense as hell. But the diorama does not end. I hear footsteps downstairs then up the stairs and finally through the door. Policemen yell at me but I'm too numb to comply. Someone grabs my shoulder and I turn to see fire. The house is on fire. There are no cops in the room that I can see. The fire starts burning the bodies of my brother and wife. I feel I should flee to safety but I move slowly, and I as walk down the stairs, I touch the flames with my hand and they don't hurt me. I take my time but eventually make it out of the house. I stand in the middle of the street and I watch it all burn. The house I bought for her now crumbles to ashes with her inside.

The intensity of the diorama distracts me for a moment from the fact all these surreal things happened in it. A briefcase turned into a knife. The cops vanished. The house burned down for no reason. I look around the neighborhood and see all lights in all houses are out. No one is even peeking out to see what the hell is going on. No curious onlookers to watch the house burn down. My hands are even clean now.

Then it hits me. This diorama is an amalgam of reality and fantasy. There is no doubt this poor man's wife slept with his brother but maybe he didn't kill them. Maybe he just walked away, fell to alcoholism and never recovered. Maybe he just fantasized about killing them.

Oh my god. We're going to be so obscenely rich. Yeah. I see it now. We came up with the technology to catch lucid dioramas. I smile and look down at my hands. There are hundred-dollar bills, rolls of them. Millions of dollars, it seems. Piles of money on the street. By the car. By the burning house.

Wait. Hold on.

With a quick thought the house goes back to normal. Another and it's daylight. I stare at the car and it turns into an expensive hyper sportscar.

We can make lucid, fully interactive dioramas. How did this happen? Oh shit. That homicidal blind rage. It was all me. I was given a starting scenario and I built the rest. Those crazy thoughts. All that rage. All that violence, it was all me. Man, am I fucked up. At least I'll have plenty of money to pay for therapy and thought-correction medication.

An idea comes to me so I look down the street and away in the distance, a grey alien pops up to existence out of nowhere. Holy shit. We're going to be so insanely rich. The archetypical grey alien from Roswell fame walks towards me and waves his hand. Where did it come from, though?

"Hey dude, what's up?" he asks with a smile in his small mouth. Huge black, unsettling eyes look at me, waiting for an answer.

"Uhh," how does one greet an alien. Well, who cares, it's not like it's real. "I'm great, how about yourself?"

"Bro, I don't know about you but I hate this hot weather."

An alien complaining about California summer. What the hell?

"Yeah…" I say. Am I talking to myself right now? Whose voice is it? Who's giving it a script? This was obviously not part of my wino friend's memory, certainly not mine either. Why does he sound like a frat boy? "Shouldn't you be speaking in some sort of weird alien language?"

"Huh?" the alien mumbles and looks at me, somehow his alien face is capable of expressing confusion much like a human's would.

"Yeah, you're from another planet, so why do you speak English?" I insist. "You know, that's why I hated Stargate SG-1, because every planet they went to, everyone spoke English without a plot reason for it. Put a science-fiction babel fish in the script or something for fucks' sakes. That's just lazy writing."

"Yeah dude, I totally get it," the grey alien says then takes a puff from a blunt that wasn't there before. "Writers, man, bunch of entitled fucks. Ohh look at me, I can type shit on a piece of paper, give me money," he says mockingly.

I chuckle at the absurdity of the scene. "No, but seriously, where did you come from?"

"Look, bro, I'm going to be honest with you," the alien says and flicks the blunt to the sidewalk. "I could answer that question with whatever bullshit comes to the head of the entitled fuck putting words in my mouth, but why bother if the diorama will end in about 10 seconds."

"What? You know you're a fictional character in a diorama?"

"I know right?" he giggles stupidly like a stereotypical stoner would. "Some trippy fourth-wall breaking meta going on right here."

"Huh?" I ask and before I can follow that up, reality warps around me.

8

The Business Plan

I wake up from the hobo's diorama feeling hung over. My head hurts. My eyeballs hurt. Still dizzy, I remove the Oneiros visor from my head and look up from the couch to see Lucy standing there.

"Well?" she asks, arms crossed. "You were crying and hyperventilating."

I reach for my face and find fresh tears I wipe off. I could explain what just happened, but no, Lucy loves surprises. It'd be fun if she finds out for herself. I look down my robe and say "good, you didn't molest me."

"Ugh," she scoffs and rolls her eyes.

"It's hard to explain," I say, getting up and placing the visor on the sofa armrest. "You better see for yourself."

"What do you mean? Is it good?"

Must hide excitement. "Yeah it is, try it."

"Well, alright," she says and takes my place in the sofa and puts the visor on. "You were joking but I'm serious, stay away from me while I'm out."

"I'm hurt you'd think so poorly of me," I say sarcastically as I sit in her nerd throne. "You ready?"

"Yeah."

The diorama file is already loaded in the Oneiros player so all I have to do is click the 'Start' button. I hear the fans speeding up in Lucy's computer. Looks like replaying these lucid dioramas takes a lot of processing power. The workstation seems beefy enough that it should handle it. Lucy, on the other hand, goes limp and lies there passed out. I let her enjoy the immersion and go to the kitchen to grab a soda. The first level of the fridge is full of ginger ale and diet cola cans. I push some of them aside to look towards the back and I'm surprised to find a couple bottles of mineral water. I pull one out of the fridge and notice the 'best by' date is a year away. Looks like she purchased it recently, just for me. How thoughtful of her.

I get back to the living room and sit in the nerd throne, observing Lucy in silence. There's a possibility these lucid dioramas are so intense some people might not be able to handle them so I bring up a 911 dialing website in her computer in case I see her convulsing. So far she seems fine. After a few minutes I see what she meant. She lies there, breathing heavily but I don't see tears running down from under the visor. Well, I guess I'm some kind of little bitch who can't help but get emotional when stabbing two dear people to death.

There was something unique to the immersion. In a typical, static rama, the scene plays exactly as it was caught from the dreamer. Experiences are full sensory immersions, that's for sure, but one retains one's personality through it. I could react to for example, a rama caught from a soldier who dreamed about a battlefield and I would feel fear, excitement or whatever but these were my reactions to what I was experiencing. Lucid rama on the other hand, I felt what the dreamer felt. I took it personal and it felt like I had intimately known these people I was stabbing. That's what intensified the experience, I figure. The stakes were high. I knew I was immersing but that didn't make the feelings any less real.

Some more minutes go by and I hear Lucy wake up. Her arms move about drunkenly, searching for the visor. That confusion will go away shortly. She finally finds and takes it off then immediately sits upright.

"Owww," she whines and reaches for her head.

Just like she did when I woke up, I stand next to her, arms crossed.

"Well, what do you think?" I ask.

Her breathing is still fast and she looks at me for a moment then down at her feet. She doesn't say a word. I guess she's still processing the fact we've struck gold.

"You understand what this means, right?" I ask.

"Yeah," she mumbles. "We found a way to make dioramas that can be controlled in real time. Like lucid dreaming."

"Yup," I nod with a wide smile and she looks up and smiles meekly. "So, did you kill the fuckers?"

"Kill them?" she asks confused. "Oh... no I did not."

Interesting. Am I really that fucked up and my only reaction to seeing my rama wife and brother fucking is murderous rage? Someone more normal would talk to them and work out the situation.

"No, I..." she continues, looking down. "I took my clothes off and joined them. We... uhm... we had a threesome."

She says this as I was taking a sip of mineral water I spit out and laugh at the remark.

"Shut up!" she exclaims, embarrassed out of her mind. "It's not funny."

"It is funny," I say with a wide grin. "And kind of hot now that I think about it."

"Ugh" she once again rolls her eyes. "Why does everything have to be a joke to you?"

"Okay, okay I'm sorry," I say and kneel on the carpet so we can be at the same eye level. "Whatever your experience was, we don't have to talk about it. But look, this is revolutionary, what we accomplished."

She seems comforted and looks at me with a shy smile. "Yeah and we weren't even coordinating to make a lucid catcher."

"I know! Isn't that awesome?"

She sits there, hands to the sides and now visibly relaxed. "Yeah, that's why the wave pattern was unique after each simulated playback. The simulator software wouldn't know what to do with a lucid rama so it just generated garbage every time. I mean, the synaptic load was..."

"Hey, hey," I interrupt and we lock eyes. "We're going to be obscenely rich," I whisper.

"Yes," she says. "Yes!"

For an instant, biting her lip, she gives me this look like a lion looking at prey then without warning jumps off the sofa to kiss me. The force of her landing pushes me to fall on my back with her on top.

"Woah Lucy, what the fuck?" I ask between chuckles.

"Shut up."

'Yes ma'am' I think to myself and return her kiss, as my hands go about undressing her.

*

We lay on our backs in silence, fully naked, on the floor of Lucy's living room. A few minutes after climax go by and she gets close to put her head on my chest. I run my arm around her back and we hold each other tightly. Such a simple gesture and it strikes me I didn't know how much I missed it. She puts her leg on mine and the warmth of her inner thighs almost burns against my skin.

"It was so strange," she says dead serious. "Having sex as a man. It was disturbing."

"I wouldn't think it's that bad."

"It's not like it was disgusting or anything," she clarifies. "It's just so different the way a man's mind works during it."

This picks my curiosity. Sex is sex. How different can it be for either gender? I make a mental note of catching a lucid female rama so I can experience the difference for myself. "Good," I say. "We'll have a target audience for such a thing. Transsexuals will pay top dollar."

"Is money the only thing you ever think about?" she asks but does so with more disappointment than annoyance in her voice. She speaks softly. Almost melancholically so.

"I'm sorry," I say, modulating my voice closer to hers. Maybe I should drop the greedy asshole act for a bit, at least until the after-sex daze wears off. "It's just so exciting. Imagine the possibilities. Anyone could be a good dreamer, we wouldn't even need to rely on rama celebrities to get started."

Lucy continues to hold on to me as if for dear life. Reminds me of how much of a fuck up I am. Breaking up with her for no real reason. Too scared of things getting too serious? Bullshit. No, so fucked up I am that I did it for fun. To hurt her, like many others had hurt me before her. Just to get that rush. That feeling of being in control over someone else's happiness. To have power and use it.

We lie in there for what feels like an hour. Lucy happens to have motion-sensing light switches and eventually they turn off. We silently agree to lie there, holding on to each other. No need to talk about anything else. No need to explain or justify what just happened between us. Just two people embracing in each other's warmth for no other reason than enjoying it. She falls asleep on me. I feel her body go limp and breathing slow down. I have no idea what time it is but I'm exhausted and so I relax and eventually fall asleep too.

*

My body shakes itself out of sleep as I keep thinking I'm going to be late for work. The temporary disorientation subsides and I remember what happened last night. Fuck, my back hurts. Last night it was a romantic thing to fall asleep in each other's embrace but now I realize sleeping on the floor was probably not the best idea. Lucy still sleeps with her face against my chest. She looks relaxed. Maybe even happy. I feel muscle cramps coming and the dried-up bodily fluids caked on our lower halves become too unbearable. I can't just push her off me so instead I gently kiss her forehead. She wakes up and meet my eyes with a smile.

"Good morning," I say gently, almost whispering.

"Hey there," she replies then continues using me as a body pillow.

"Hey... I have to email the boss man."

"Oh yeah, sorry," she says and sits up. I take a few seconds to admire her body. Lucy is not exactly athletic but I wouldn't call her fat either. She's got meat on her bones. More of a full body, really. Just my type. I get a hard on just staring at her but stop myself. We have business to attend to. Lucy turns to look at me in all my obese 250-pound naked glory and giggles as she stands up.

"What?" I say, faking outrage. "You fail to appreciate my unique physique."

She ignores the comment and picks up her clothes, walks to the room and locks the door behind her. A few seconds later, I hear she's taking a shower. I don't have any clothes so I just put the bathrobe back on. Lucy's nerd throne is one of those 'gaming' chairs with built in speakers in the headrest. It's very comfortable. I should get myself one of these. In her computer, I open a web browser and login to my Dreamax email account and type a quick bullshit excuse to not come in to the office. Something about feeling under the weather. I CC Linda from HR in case Scott misses it. There, no more obligations from me and I still get paid.

After a while, Lucy comes out of the room wearing her own white bathrobe.

"Hey, let's do breakfast," I say. "We have much to discuss."

"Listen, what happened last night," ugh here we go, back to clichéd girl-speak.

"Don't worry, I get it." I say. "I mean, we have a business to build."

"Yeah," she says, biting her lower lip. "Okay, I'll get dressed. What about you?"

"We'll stop by my place to drop off the shit water clothes and get fresh ones."

"Alright."

*

We left my place not too long ago. I got to take a shower myself and get dressed too. I threw the bag with the shit water clothes in the trash container. Lucy has been quiet ever since we left her place. She's probably regretting last night but I don't mind. She's probably thinking about the sentimental implications and whatnot. I think about that stuff too but damn, why can't an impulse fuck be just that and nothing else to women?

I'm driving to a coffee house a few blocks away. They have desks and free WiFi for the cash strapped entrepreneur who wishes to run a business from there. Not a bad deal. In exchange, they get to sell $10 coffee. I park nearby and exit the car. Lucy follows. The damn trash bag I put on the seat is uncomfortable but at least fresh clothes won't be ruined by it. It's starting to annoy me how quiet she is. We get to the front door and I open it for her. We go in and order whatever fancy named coffee, milk and artificial flavoring concoction they have on sale for the season. Then we sit down and I open my laptop.

"Okay, sorry to push but what's going on?" I ask, knowing it's not the best idea as she hates being pressured.

Lucy takes a sip of her warm coffee and looks away. "I don't want to go through it all over again is all."

"Look, one thing led to the next. We were both probably feeling lonely or something and-"

"So it was just a spontaneous fuck then?"

"Yeah," I say. Must carefully measure words. Talking to women about relationship stuff is like defusing a nuclear bomb. "I mean, I think so. Do you?"

"I guess," she says, staring at nothing in particular.

"We can discuss it later. Can we please talk about the historical breakthrough we just built?"

She smiles and finally, snaps out of it. "Alright."

"Great," I say, returning the smile. "So, what we have here is a new class of diorama. Something that has never been done before. I don't think we can even call them dioramas anymore."

"Lucid Diorama," Lucy says as if testing the words out loud. "Liorama? Lucirama?"

"That sounds terrible."

"I know," she says, chuckling.

"Catchy names aside, do you know how it happened?"

"Well, I'm hoping it's not a one-time thing caused by the wino's mental state or whatever combination of medication and alcohol he was in at the time of the catch. Could be some brains or certain mental states are ripe for a full neural catch."

"Full neural catch?" I ask. I like how those words mix together.

"Yeah," she explains. Thank god the awkwardness of impulse sex is gone and now she's back at her know-it-all usual self. "A traditional catch is initiated at a neural entry point provided by the dreamer by focusing on the particular memory. We don't really understand what happens in the brain when we do this. It's almost as if the dreamer retrieves the target diorama from neural archive memory consciously. Then, a dreamcatcher takes a brainwave snapshot which can then be reproduced in a powerful enough computer for the memory to be relived in full sensory form. This is when the diorama is ready for consumer immersion."

Damn. That was a mouthful and she didn't even take a sip of coffee once. It's why she caught my attention all those months ago. Cute and sharp as hell. The complete package. I nod every now and then through her explanation and when she's done, I ask "what makes this one lucid then? What set it apart?"

"I'm hoping it had nothing to do with the wino's brain and it was all about the prototype dream catcher. I built the firmware as efficiently as humanly possible and in turn, you took advantage of efficient coding to make the catch process much faster. I think it's the way you built it. The location of the brainwave sensors and the power output. Might have been blind luck for all I know. It seems to me the prototype snapshots not just a memory but a full neural state. A full catch all around."

"Huh," I mumble. "A full catch diorama."

"Now that sounds stupid."

"No, it doesn't. It sounds cool like the title of a 90's anime or maybe an indie science fiction novel a whole dozen people might read."

"Whatever," Lucy says, taking a sip of her coffee.

"Anyway, I'm thinking the setting in this rama we got is generic enough that couldn't be traced to our anonymous business partner."

"Stop calling him that," she says, annoyed. "It's bad enough we used and dumped him in an alley when were done with him."

"Fair enough. Our 'dreamer', then," I say, placing emphasis on the word and abstaining from reminding her I did pay him for services rendered. "I'm too excited about this. I want to unleash our full catch diorama to the world at large."

"I could build a showcase website for it. But the question is, how are we going to monetize it?"

"I'm thinking we host your website on pirate distributed hosting, accessible only through TOR, then I put a bitcoin plugin in it to charge people," I explain the master plan as I pull the smartphone out of my pocket and do a web search. "Let's seeeeee… bitcoin still leads the cryptocurrency pack in popularity and the price has been stable enough for the last year at $2,376, give or take a few dollars."

"Tax evasion added to the list of laws we've been breaking," Lucy says, making a checkmark gesture with her right hand.

I scoff and put the phone back and say "if you think modern technology giants made it big by following the rules, I have bad news for you. And if you're done, I'd like to get back to your place and start building our empire."

Once again, Lucy is back at that tensed up state so I add, "we'll be working only. I swear, no more naked stuff."

She nods, apparently relieved and stands up. I feel like reminding her she is the one who initiated last night's 'naked stuff' but fine, I'll let it go and pretend I was just fulfilling my role as the creepy guy forcing myself onto a sweet innocent butterfly or a woman incapable of a single impure thought.

*

Lucy has been working her keyboard frenetically as usual for the last couple hours while I sit in the couch going over the bitcoin stuff. I created a wallet, confirmed it belongs in the blockchain and can take incoming payments.

"Hey Lucy," I say, looking up from my laptop. She turns her nerd throne to face me and I ask "how much do you think we should charge for each download."

"Uhm…" she mumbles, looking away as if putting some real thought into it. "We want to keep them cheap so people in less developed countries buy into it too. Our priority right now should be to establish a customer base. We can bump the prices later."

"Marketing genius over here," I say with a smile. Fuck, that's a good point. "Say, 99 cents?"

"Sounds about right," she says with a nod.

"Agreed. The plugin will charge whatever the local currency equivalent is in bitcoin when they confirm the purchase."

Lucy turns her chair to continue working. I buy in-game currency in an obscure Korean MMORPG[1] then sell it to a player offering bitcoin, which in turn I use to purchase a domain for our nascent empire. Good look tracing it back to who purchased fullcatchdiorama.com, NSA. I add www.fullcatchdiorama.com too because not all boomers have died off and some people still think you have to have a 'www' to go 'surf the information superhighway.'

In the middle of covering my illicit tracks, I look up and stare at Lucy for a moment, maybe wishing she gets in the mood like last night. Maybe it was an altered state of mind caused by full catch diorama immersion, something not likely to happen again. Back when we were dating she was somewhat cold and distant and it was usually up to me to figure out how to get her going. Last night was a god damn surprise I don't think either of us saw coming. On the other hand, I did not wake up from diorama full of murderous rage. It could be the alien dude at the end calmed me down enough to get back to normal and she just didn't get that sort of a buffer. If these things get as popular as I think they will,

---

[1] Editor's note: MMORPG stands for Massive Multiplayer Online Roleplaying Game. A type of fantasy second life online game with a large player population and its own self-contained economy. Some players engage in RMT (Real Money Trading), exchanging real world and in-game currency outside of the game.

millions of people may be soon walking around dazed and confused.

Eh… there's already a legion of anti-depressant addicted, oversocialized social media slaves out there. Things wouldn't be that much different.

9

Moving On To Other Opportunities

I have a love-hate relationship with coffee. On the one hand, I do appreciate the flavor despite its bitterness. On the other, well, coffee makes me jittery and emotional. I avoid it as much as I can, especially when I know I'm going to be tested on my ability to keep my cool, like a job interview or public speaking. But today, I'm too hammered, having slept only three hours after spending a long evening coding like crazy at Lucy's apartment. We didn't even fuck again but at least we got the marketplace going. We still have to figure out marketing, translations, international markets and new content but it's a good start.

The Dreamax lunch room feels so empty. It's 9:15 AM and there should be at least a dozen slaves chatting away the first couple hours of their workday. Fascinating discussions about fantasy football and the latest Instagram trend should be overheard around the room, but instead I'm by myself, adding a second sugar substitute packet to my mug. Oh well, less PDF readers to install, I suppose.

It's a day not much different than any other. Steve hasn't poked me yet. The boss man usually comes around this time to discuss the daily list of PDF reader installations and whatever else will keep me busy for the day. Maybe he figured I'm still recovering from yesterday's 'sickness'. I'm typing some ticket reports and already can feel my hands subtly shaking as the effects of the caffeine kick in. Boy, I sure hope nothing stressful happens today.

"Helloooooo…" says Linda from HR in her distinctive acute vocal fry, forcing me to look up past the wall of my cubicle. Just the tone of her high-pitched screeching voice slightly enrages me. I can feel my right eyelid twitching but must remain calm. Must promote synergy and all that.

"Hey, Linda. How can I help you?"

"Good morning, Teeeeeed. I heard you weren't feeling very well yessssterdaaayyyyy," she says with the widest, fakest smile she seems capable of mustering.

"Yeah," I say, reclining back on my chair, giving myself a little massage on the belly. "Guess I ate something that had been dead for too long."

Lifestyle vegetarians. Too easy to push their buttons. I see the faintest sign the fake smile might drop but by God she has the temperament of a bull and keeps it up, then says, "oh no! I hope you're feeling better now!"

"Yeah, I am, thanks. Nothing like a bottle of Pepto and easy access to the restroom to get it all out."

"I'm so happy to hear thaaaaaaat," she says, tilting her head to the side like puppies do. Makes me wonder if puppies learned it from people or, since people find the gesture cute, they appropriated it from the animals. "Say, could you come to my office for a minute?"

"Oh, I'm very sorry but I'm in the middle of something. But feel free to open a ticket and we'll get right back at you."

"No worries, it's not a computer probleeeeeeeem."

Huh. Impromptu invitation to the HR office. I wonder if that one Adderall fan club cheerleader upstairs reported me for sexual harassment for the one time our eyes met from 20 feet away in the lunch room for 2 seconds. Guys have been fired and careers ruined for less than that. #MeToo, #BelieveWomen. Oh well, not like I'll need a job in a couple weeks anyway.

The HR office is a short walk away from the IT nerds general area. I follow Linda and she goes in first. Before I even step in, I see Paul from Loss Prevention and Steve already there. Waiting for me. Oh fuck. My hands start shaking a little faster. I hope it's not noticeable.

"Please take a seaaaat," Linda says and points to a chair in front of her desk. Steve sits in another right next and Paul chills comfortably in the sofa against the wall.

"Hey guys," I greet them with an innocent smile and sit down. They mumble something in return.

"I'm going to take the lead heeere gentlemen," says Linda. I look to the side to see if Steve is as annoyed by the vocal fry but he simply looks at me and nods. "Ted, it has come to our attentioooon that a certain piece of hardwareeee is missing from the catch shoooop."

"Oh no," I say, holding a hand to my mouth in shock. It's obvious they know it was me and they have evidence to prove it. I want to fuck with them for a bit but I'm too stupefied by caffeine overload.

I hear Paul sighing behind me, perhaps due to the smell of bullshit, then I turn my chair when he says "yes, and we have logs showing that you initiated a flood attack from a server, targeting the IP camera covering the catch chair from where its neural scanner disappeared."

"Not only that," says Steve, taking his turn. "We see you in the cameras going to the shop, then exiting while the video feed was interrupted. As soon as you get back to your desk, you type something in your computer and the IP camera goes back to normal."

"Wait, am I a suspect?" I ask. I refrain from asking for a lawyer.

"Let's all calm dooooooown," says Linda. "You can imagine the position we're iiiiiin. The evidence suggests you may have... erm... borrowed equipment that belongs to the companyyyyyy."

The effects of the coffee cup appear to become amplified. But I don't fight it. I let my body tremble to the concoction of caffeine, sugar and adrenaline rushing through my veins. I let it show. "Well, that's just not fair," I say and hear my own voice crack. "I went to the lunch room to get a soda and now you're calling me a thief?"

"We're not calling you anything. At least not yet," says Paul from behind me. The guy puts so much effort on making his voice sound authoritative. Poor wannabe police who probably failed academy and now gets the consolation prize of being a corporate Loss Prevention loon. "But we'll be conducting a thorough investigation."

"Listen, Ted," says Scott and I look at him. "I believe you had nothing to do with this, but we have to follow corporate procedures in these cases. I mean, a pretty expensive piece of equipment disappeared and we need to figure out how."

"S-so what happens to me now?" I ask Linda, voice shaking.

"I'm very sorry Teeeed. We'll put you on administrative leaveeeee and replace your hourly wages with accrued vacation timeeeeee."

"I don't believe this," I say, looking down to my feet. "We've been through so much. All the things we've done and now you show me the door. I thought Dreamax was my family."

Paul scoffs behind me. "Dude, please, you're embarrassing yourself."

"What do you mean?" I ask looking at him. "What does he mean?" I ask Linda from HR.

"Please calm down Ted," Linda says, grabbing my hand. I see tears forming in her eyes. Fuck, at least the vocal fry appears under control. "I apologize. You'll be very welcome back once the investigation is cleared."

I nod meekly. I hear Paul stand up behind me and puts a hand on my shoulder and says "let's go, buddy."

"What about my stuff? I have personal things in my desk drawers."

"LP will go through it then I'll put everything in a box and ship to your address on record," says Linda, sniffling.

I nod again. Meekly. Then Paul guides me out of the HR office, past the bullpen and through the stairs down to the first floor. The small number of NPCs that remain at Dreamax HQ look up from their boring work days, give me a quick glance and return to their conversations about fantasy football and the 'insta.'

"Alright, buddy, we'll be in touch," says Paul then closes the door behind me.

I turn around and look at my former place of employment. I'll miss the free diorama screenings, I guess. It's only 10:30 AM so I make my way to the coffee shop a couple blocks away. The email account and admin access in my smartphone have already been blocked. Scott probably clicked a button the minute he saw Linda take me to the HR office. As I walk the short distance, I login to my bitcoin purse and see a whole whooping $33 and 33 cents in transactions. Some people have already started purchasing the wino's rama. Just have to wait for it to go viral and we'll be set.

No more coffee. I go inside the coffee house and order an orange juice. As I scan for a free seat, waiting for them to mix pulp concentrate with tap water, I text Lucy.

From Me:
How's sales?

No answer. I get my order first, before I even see the three dots in the SMS app and sit down. There is no rush. I take a breath to enjoy the smell of forbidden bean juice and exhale. I savor freedom from corporate slavery. I must remember this day. I wonder how future generations will think of me. Will they call me the Steve Jobs of entertainment? The Edison of the diorama. A genius. A visionary. A captain of industry. Sweet immortality, here I come.

I feel my phone vibrate inside my pocket, pull it out and read Lucy's response.

> From Lucy:
> Not good. 33 sales in the first 2 hours the site went live then nothing in the last 8 hours.

Fuck, that's not good. Eight hours is too old for a meme to go viral.

> From Me:
> Did you promote in the chans like I told you?

> From Lucy:
> Yes, and I was told "not your personal army" and "tits or GTFO"

This is not good. Not good at all. Immortality slips through my fingers. I don't understand, someone in those 33 purchases should have tweeted it to a rama e-celebrity. Where is the buzz? How do you advertise illegal content to the masses?

> From Me:
> Thx, I'll think of something

Even if I'm not out of a job, I can't go back to a cubicle now. Just when I thought I was out, the NPCs pull me back in. I take a few sips of OJ, allowing myself a few seconds of silence in my head to clear my mind. And it comes to me. If the masses want celebrities, celebrities they shall have. My phone still has a cached, outdated version of the Dreamax corporate contacts list. I find the man's email address and compose a message, short but to the point.

```
From: Ted Davies (tedsseract@tormail.es)
To: Topher Bass (tobogan@dream.ax)
Subject: Business opportunity

How would you like to be the next Chad
Mars?
-Ted
```

There goes nothing. Who knows how loyal the Maximum Straya is to Dreamax? But I haven't even put the phone down when it vibrates with a new message. ToBogan is interested and he's giving me his cell phone number. I copy-paste it into the phone's contact books then send him a text.

```
                              From Me:
                    Are you still in LA?
```

He replies almost immediately.

```
From ToBogan:
Yah
```

```
                              From Me:
                          Can we talk?
```

```
From ToBogan:
now?
```

```
                                       From Me:
                                       Yah
```

Might be pushing it but now it's not the time for subtleties. If anything, it may convey a sense of urgency. Who wouldn't want to be the next Chad Mars? The phone vibrates again with an address in Santa Monica. A GPS app points to a boardwalk parking lot. Worst that can happen is he laughs at my proposal. Even then, I'll take the opportunity to eat some beach hotdogs.

10

Third Wheel

I make it to the boardwalk less than half hour later, even after having to walk home to get the car. Got to love those empty LA freeways. I used to come here with my family when I was little for birthdays and other special occasions. Nothing would beat the seafood places, ice cream shop and the arcade on the pier. You could walk a short distance away from the water to find street performers and masses of tourists and rich assholes showing off their million-dollar supercars.

Santa Monica was somewhat spared the brunt of the crash. It's still got some tourist value and as far as I know, most of the condos near the water are still occupied. Most owned by Saudi and Chinese nationals. I don't see many of either but street signs and stores mostly incorporate Mandarin and Arabian characters in signage and logos. There used to be a few beach bums here and there but the Chinese don't fuck around. Some city ordinance was passed years ago to forcibly remove loiterers that usually get dumped a few blocks inside the city of Los Angeles.

I have no problem finding a parking spot by the boardwalk, among extravagant golden and red luxury vehicles and the occasional high-end Kia here and there. Even before I get out of the car, I see a small crowd gathering by the beach gym. Bunch of swings, ropes, benches and other artifacts for the fitness-obsessed to publicly show off the fruit of their steroids investments. Or in this case, a mildly relevant rama dreamer in a green and gold speedo.

ToBogan. The Top Bogan. The Maximum Straya. He hangs from gymnastics still rings doing swings and turns and other tricks. Easy to forget before he became famous for poking deadly Australian outback beasts assholes, Topher Bass was already well known in a couple sports disciplines. Good enough to win local tournaments but never to make it to the Olympics. Good enough, but not quite to win first place. Something I can exploit, I figure.

I stand by the edge of the small crowd. An odd mix of Chinese and Saudi women from the neighborhood. The former group mostly wearing those bikini sets that cover a good couple square inches of skin they might as well be naked and the latter, full black gowns you can only see their eyes. Away from the circle of swooning fans wetting themselves to the sight of such a virile alpha male specimen, their men stand around or mind the children. Nothing stranger than Americanized fundamentalist cultures.

The show goes on for a few minutes and I get bored and walk away to sit in a nearby bench. I nod to a middle-aged Chinese dude smoking an e-cig there, no doubt waiting for his woman to be finished cuckholding him in public. Some more twists and turns and spins and ToBogan finishes by rapidly spinning, letting go of the rings, then landing and making a pose, as sand raises up in the air. The small crowd gasps and claps then rush him to get autographs and maybe steal a squeeze of those sun-tanned muscles. As he signs little pieces of paper, we lock eyes for a moment and he gives me a 'be right there' look.

About half hour later, he's finally done pleasing the fans. I see some of them grab their men and rush them away, perhaps back to the privacy of their expensive beachside condos before the heat of arousal fades away.

"Out to make me the next Chad Mars, are you?" says ToBogan, as he sits next to me. The man still wears nothing but the tiny speedo emblazoned with the colors of his motherland. There's a white towel on his shoulders he uses to wipe some of the sweat away.

"That's right," I say with a nod. It's a good thing the bench is wide enough so I can sit far away enough as to avoid the sweaty smell.

Topher Bass chuckles and leaves the towel alone, reclining back and running his left arm along the back of the bench then says with a wide grin "and how do you plan to do that?"

Here it comes. All or nothing. I turn slightly to my right so I can see him in the eyes and ask him "what made Chad Mars so famous? What's the difference between you and him?"

The Maximum Straya smiles no more. "Hard to compete with a trust fund baby. The guy came out of nowhere with millions of dollars to do his exotic holiday ramas while I was still busy with gymnastics." I quickly realize his loud, exaggerated bogan accent is all part of his rama persona, as he now talks in normal American English, pretty much indistinguishable from a native speaker's.

"Wrong," I say with the deepest voice I can make without looking like an attempt to be threatening. "Chad Mars was not the first to a relatively new platform but knew exactly how to use it to its maximum potential. Just like Stan Lee or Shigeru Miyamoto or Pewdiepie"

ToBogan listens attentively, every now and then looking around the beach at nothing in particular, if only to break eye contact for a moment. Discussing Chad Mars is apparently an uncomfortable subject for this alpha male specimen. He does not interrupt, while I continue my sales pitch.

"Chad Mars did not come out of nowhere. True, he is a trust fund baby, but he made a name for himself in the darknet fetish scene. All he had to do was realize the potential of the diorama, a new platform the old dinosaurs in the legacy entertainment industries of music, movies, videogames and VR scoffed at. And now, where are the Hollywood blockbusters? Where are the videogames that players used to rabidly preorder? The singers who used to fill stadiums? The VR experiences? Gone, no one gives a shit about that crap anymore. It's all about the ramas now."

"So, you're saying you invented something better than a rama?" the Straya asks, sea breeze making a mess of hair coated in dried sweat.

"I can't talk much about it without you agreeing to be the third partner in a startup," I say.

A smile comes back to ToBogan's. He crosses his arms to his chest and says "Dreamax pays me 20 mil a year, whether their ramas sell or not. What makes you think I'd leave that behind in exchange for your vague promises?"

I return the smile plus a shrug. "It'll be a leap of faith. Do you think Chad Mars makes 20 mil a year?"

ToBogan scoffs again, his grin reduced to a smile trying to hide annoyance. This is where I stop calling the name of his greatest rival. We sit there for several minutes, as I let the Straya digest the conversation and think for a bit. I don't mind waiting, it's been years since the last time I came to the beach. A real beach. Although at the end of the day there is no sensory difference between real and rama.

"I'll give you a couple hours to show me, what the hell," he finally breaks the silence.

"I need your signature in an NDA first," I say, summoning superhuman strength to not show excitement. I then pull up a NDA form in my smartphone and hand it to him for e-signature.

Without hesitation, he takes it from my hand, places his finger on the thumbprint reader then gives it back. "Alright then let's go make me the next Chad Mars."

I make a gesture with my eyes towards his exposed bulge.

"Oh right," he says with a chuckle. "Clothes are over there, give me 10 minutes."

*

"The fuck's that smell?" the Straya asked when we got in my car. I explained I had tripped into some disgusting sewage pool by accident and didn't have a choice but to drive home while soaked in the ungodly concoction. We opened the windows all the way down and this provided some relief for him and also for me, as there was no further opportunity for him to keep asking any more questions about the 'new technology' due to the noise of the wind circulating in and out.

Eventually we make it to North Hollywood, then Lucy's street. Again, I have to park a couple blocks away. ToBogan wears sunglasses and a baseball cap to mask his identity. Like anyone gives a shit about him. Oh, but they will. They will, big time.

I knock the door to Lucy's apartment. She opens a couple seconds later. A new record, as she usually takes her god damn time when I visit. But no, I texted her in advance I was bringing ToBogan himself. She grins like few times I've seen then hugs me, then hugs him then urges us to come in. She even hastily cleaned up her mess. A celebrity is in the house.

"Did you guys talk about it?" Lucy asks us, after we sit down in her couch.

"Vaguely," grunts ToBogan.

"Well, surely you understand…" I begin.

"Yeah, yeah. I signed the damn thing, will you show me now, please?"

"Yeah, for sure. Better if you see for yourself," I say, standing up and motioning for him to lay down on the couch.

Instead, ToBogan grabs the Oneiros visor and looks at me, disappointment in his face then says "really? It's just a rama."

"A new class of rama," I say, still motioning for him to lay down. "Sorry, that's all I can say."

For a few seconds ToBogan looks at the visor, then at me, then at Lucy, then back at the visor. My heart races. He seems to be considering just walking out of there. In the end, he shrugs, maybe he figures all he was going to lose was 10 minutes of dreaming a rama. He takes off the baseball hat and lays down. Lucy goes behind him to assist in putting on the Oneiros.

"Hey, don't do anything funny with my junk while I'm out, eh?" ToBogan says.

I look at Lucy and say "see? It's a legitimate request for a man too." She just rolls her eyes then sits at her nerd throne. Then she does a dramatic and unnecessary countdown from 5 and runs the full catch diorama from the hobo for him. ToBogan's body tenses for a couple seconds, then goes limp, fully immersed in next generation diorama.

Several minutes go by. ToBogan is deep in diorama sensory immersion without apparent reaction. Lucy sits in her nerd throne in silence. Sometimes looking at me, until our eyes meet for a second, then at the sleeping Straya. Whether she's still awkward about the whole impulse fuck thing or worried about him joining our business venture or not is anyone's guess.

It doesn't take long for the experience to finish and ToBogan inhales deeply then exhales, his body coming back to life. He then reaches for the Oneiros to take it off. He puts it to the side and sits up, massaging his temples with his right hand. Me and Lucy stare at him in silence, unsure of what's going on.

After a short while, I get tired of waiting for a reaction and ask "well? What do you think?"

"Huh," ToBogan mumbles then looks at me for a second. Not only was he massaging his temples, he was also wiping tears from his eyes and they're still red from moisture. "Fucking hell," is all he has to say.

I think I know what he means. I think he gets it. "Awesome, isn't it?"

"Yeah," he says, looking at me, then Lucy. "Yeah."

The Maximum Straya seems at a loss for words. He doesn't move. Doesn't talk. I try breaking the ice and ask "well, did you kill them? Or did you fuck them?"

"Really?" asks Lucy. I shrug then she rolls her eyes.

"What?" ToBogan asks, seemingly still disoriented. "Who?"

"The people in the lucid diorama you just lived," I say. "You know, that diorama, the type that's going to make us obscenely rich and yourself bigger than Chad Mars?"

"Oh," he mumbles then reclines back on the sofa. "I don't know what you're talking about. The rama started outside of a house, at night. So I went exploring the neighborhood."

"Huh," I say then me and Lucy look at each other, confused.

"I just walked down the street," he continues. "It was dark. It was… sad. I just kept walking and walking until I reached the edge of the stage. This is when I realized it was a lucid rama. Simply by walking beyond the limits that were caught from the dreamer."

"Isn't it awesome? Lucid dioramas!" I say with a wide grin. ToBogan is still deathly serious. It begins to disturb me, as I've never seen him in this sustained state of misery.

"Yeah," he says.

"Well, then what happened?" asked Lucy, maybe asserting her role as the other business partner so we don't forget.

"This lucid diorama. It creates weird shit the moment you think about it," he says, looking at me.

"Tell me about it," I say. "I ended up with a self-aware pothead alien friend."

ToBogan nods in acknowledgement then says "these creations, they get pulled from your memory. Some kind of mix between diorama and your memories and the dreamer's."

"Sure," I say. "I probably saw that pothead alien in a movie or a cartoon when I was little. What did you see?"

"Shit I didn't want to remember," he says.

Not good, it dug up some traumatic shit. What could be so traumatic for such a specimen of alpha maleness though?

"At least not this... vividly," he adds, looking down at the floor.

I sit there, letting him take his time to process. Not only will these dioramas be raw, vivid, lucid dreams on demand but, if they can force you to relive traumatic events, maybe there will be some use in psychiatry. Fuck, if these can fix people's inner fucked-up-ness, we could make so much more money on medical insurance claims alone. Got to figure out a way to get them endorsed by whatever scammy psychiatry association is out there.

"I can see what you mean," the Straya eventually says, looking me in the eyes. "New platform, new class of diorama. Whoever gets their name out there first will monopolize the market at least for a few months."

"Exactly," I say, big grin on my face.

"Yeah," he relaxes and returns the smile. "Let's do it."

"Alright!" exclaims Lucy from her nerd throne.

"So how does it work?" asks ToBogan.

"Here," I say and pick up the catcher, which Lucy by now has installed in new bicycle helmet-looking casing.

"This is it?" asks ToBogan skeptically. "This is your dreamcatcher?"

"Yep," I say smugly. "Compact design, super-fast catch, wireless and relatively painless. Not to mention it catches lucid dioramas."

The Maximum Straya picks up the 'catcher from my hand and observes it for a moment, and before he gets second thoughts I say "well, shall we catch a lucid diorama from that croc bitten head of yours?"

"I'll give it a shot," he says, looking at us. "But I won't be signing any papers until I see it again in action, with my own diorama. I still have exclusivity with Dreamax, you know."

"Well, you know," says Lucy. "You have contractual exclusivity to not distribute dioramas with other companies but I'm sure your contract says nothing about you distributing from your own company."

"Yeah," I add, seeing where she's going. "A company you're founding with two fellow Dreamax ex-employees."

Without comment, ToBogan nods in acknowledgement then says, "I still want to test it before I commit to anything."

"Totally understandable," I say, then motion for him to recline again on the couch. "Shall we?"

ToBogan nods and lies down, while Lucy turns her throne to type in my laptop, which still has the custom catch software on its screen. I sit in the sofa next to him and they go at it. Lucy asks him for a memory to use as entry point then does her dramatic countdown again. ToBogan again goes limp and lies there. For a moment, I recall the hobo going berserk during the catch and wonder if the same thing happens to him, he'll probably trash the place before we can stop him. He's a big guy after all. For me.

But the catch goes on uneventfully. ToBogan doesn't suffer the way he'd do with a traditional Dreamax catch. Not even five minutes pass when I see on my laptop's screen the process is completed and he wakes up as if from a nap. Maybe the hobo's mental state caused berserker mode.

Maybe his brain was unique for lucid diorama catch and ToBogan's is only going to give us a regular old rama. Fuck.

"All good," says Lucy and I look at her to see she's pointing at her screen. Apparently she's already copied over the catch to her renderer and on it, we see the same mess of seemingly random brainwaves characteristic of lucid diorama. It worked. I smile and let out a sigh in relief.

"Alright, well, I got to go to a photo shoot," ToBogan says as he gets up.

"Hey, mastering takes like an hour, you don't want to wait?" I ask.

"Nah, give me a ride back to the beach mate," he says. Maybe important celebrities such as himself only have a short tolerance for being around the nobodies for short periods of time. "Text me when it's ready and I'll come take a look."

"Alright then," I say and give Lucy a thumbs-up as I follow ToBogan out the door.

We walk the couple blocks to my car and check on our new business partner. I fail to figure out how his demeanor went from his usual bogan frat boy persona to being completely quiet. Could be he's trying to deal with the fact he's going to be the next Chad Mars. Or maybe he's annoyed because he thinks this whole evening was a waste of time. I'm driving down the 10 East and to test the waters, I ask him "well, what do you think?"

ToBogan seems lost in thought for a moment, then looks at me and says "I don't know, we'll see when it's ready for dreaming."

"You saw in the sample rama," I try to reassure him. "This is going to be huge, and you're going to be huge with it."

"Look, you don't get it," he says. "Some things buried in the back of your head are better left there."

Man's got a point. "Was it that bad?"

"It's not so much my personal temporary discomfort. How is this going to change people in general, I wonder. Suddenly, people are going to be able to look at each other's inner demons."

Damn. I didn't even think of it. If anything, raw, uncensored inner demon shit would probably be obscenely profitable. "How bad can it be?" I ask. "People used to listen to violent hip-hop and watch disgusting things online all the time and we're not in some post-apocalyptic hellhole.

"Who knows? We'll find out."

Yeah. We will. Worse comes to worse, we'll be too high up our ivory towers by the time there's riots in the streets. Kind of surprising for a veteran frat boy to care about society and its ills.

We make it back to Santa Monica eventually and I drop off ToBogan with the promise he'll come by tomorrow or the next day once the diorama is ready for dreaming. On my way back I stop by a car wash where they remove the plastic covering from the driver's seat and they attempt to detail out the increasingly disgusting smell of shit water. They take an hour going at it and eventually return it. The manager is embarrassed, there's still a faint whiff lingering inside, despite the generous amounts of lavender scent sprayed. Whatever, I'll buy a new car next week. A better one. One of those self-driving pure hydrogen with the gullwing doors. With leather seats, yeah. I pay the man for doing his best and drive off.

It's dark when I make it back to my neighborhood. Downtown LA. Homeless Central. The hobos begin forming lines along the streets leading up to the Pershing Square tent city for their free dinner. I make a right to get near my building, but I'm stopped by a police road block. I thought cops were not supposed to touch the hobos. Not that they'd want to. The three lanes of the one-way street are squeezed into one by traffic cones. Police interceptor red and blue lights illuminate the otherwise neglected street. Then I see it.

Yellow police tape blocks access to an alley. I know this alley. I slow down and continue driving past the roadblock. Police officers point flashlights by an orange trash container and the white blankets covering a mass, obviously shaped like a body.

Fuck me. I'm sure it's the same alley. Is it the same hobo? Is that our former business partner there? Did we kill him?

I continue past the scene trying to not look suspicious. Like any of the cops is going to see my face through tinted windows at that hour anyway. If that's him, I don't recall if I touched him or the trash container or any other place where my prints might be. Maybe some hair fell off my head. Maybe the hobo scratched me and kept some DNA samples under his fingernails. Then again this is a random hobo out of thousands in Downtown LA. I don't think they're going to go full CSI and waste money on someone with enough alcohol in their blood to die twice.

Past the cop cars, traffic goes back to normal and it doesn't take me long to drive into my building. I'm in a dazed state as I walk out of it and into the elevator and into my apartment and into my living room and sit in my nerd throne. Mine doesn't have speakers. I'll buy one with huge fucking ones when we start making money. When our full catch dioramas go viral. Yeah. We have two now, the hobo's as well as ToBogan. But the hobo is dead now. We'll find out soon if from alcohol poisoning or the catch job.

11

Virality

Woken up to the text message alert chime. What's the point of being let go from work if I can't sleep until my eyes hurt? I check the phone. It's Lucy.

> From Lucy:
> T's rama is ready

> From Me:
> Have you dreamt it?

> From Lucy:
> No. Come. You do first

> From Me:
> I'll get breakfast first.
> See you in a couple hours.

More like lunch. I check the clock. It's 11:49 AM. Should check on ToBogan. A text message should do it.

From Me:
Heyo

I wait 10 minutes. Nothing.

From Me:
Meet at Lucy's?

Another 10 minutes. Nothing. It bugs me to be ignored but it's also worrying, after seeing the police crime scene yesterday. Yeah, looked like a crime scene. Not just some random wino's body giving out to the excess alcohol, but an actual murder scene. Maybe it was a different hobo in the same alley. There's one way to find out.

I get out of bed. Slept naked. Hate air conditioning. Will have to wash bedcovers soon. Quick shower. Get dressed. I walk out of my building and make for the alley, five blocks away. It's noon in Downtown LA, and it's summer too. Rising temperatures and the god damn sunlight evaporate the trails of piss and shit and vomit from the sidewalks. The scents wafting in the air must be what hell smells like. At least the hobos keep to themselves. Mentally ill or not, as long as one ignores them, they're mostly harmless.

Five blocks away, into the former jewelry district, I arrive at the alley. It is still cordoned out with yellow police tape. But I don't see anyone guarding it. I take a glance down the street towards the Pershing Square tent city. Nothing. Then back in the other direction. Nothing. Police mostly keep away from homeless concentrations. Too much of a legal liability if they bump into a hobo by accident and the department gets hit with yet another abuse lawsuit. I gently lift the yellow tape above my head and walk into the alley.

There's nothing in here, besides the trash container where our former business partner indulged in his self-pleasuring activities. I look around for anything incriminating, like the cops wouldn't have found it when they canvassed the scene. Nothing. Other than the yellow tape by the sidewalk, nothing in here gives the impression someone died last night.

"Hey!" I hear a shout from the sidewalk. I turn and see a cop car. I just smile and wave the two police inside as I walk towards them.

"Hey officers," I say with a big smile.

"Lost something?" the uniformed guy riding shotgun asks.

I squint and bend a little so I can see his face and answer "nah, I live down the street and was just wondering what happened here."

"Guy died," says the cop at the wheel. I bend I little further and I can see it's some young guy, probably just out of academy.

"That sucks," I say. "Was he mugged or something? I have to walk around here at night you know."

The cop at the window scoffs. Older guy, maybe the supervisor of the kid at the wheel. Then he says "I wouldn't come out for a stroll at night. In fact, I'd move the hell out of here if I lived anywhere in a 5-mile radius."

"Nah, no mugging," says the kid at the wheel. I can't see his name badge. "Weird thing, probably one of those drugs people cook up."

"Really?" I ask.

"Yeah, the guy's brain pretty much melted to a pulp," the supervisor-type adds. "Not a pretty sight. At least he probably didn't suffer."

Fuck. Me.

"That sucks," I say, doing my best to hide distress.

"Yeah, but nothing to worry about," supervisor cop says. "I still wouldn't walk out here at night by myself."

"Thanks, officer," I say. Big smile. Must look like random guy. "Will keep that in mind."

Supervisor cop nods and tells young cop to keep driving. The car rides to the corner then makes a right and disappears from sight. I pull my phone out and try again.

From Me:
Yo, straya. Ping me when you can, will you?

I wait 10 minutes. Nothing. Fuck. Me. Don't die on me, ToBogan. We have ramas to catch.

*

Back in Lucy's neighborhood. Regardless of the day of the week I drive in here, it always feels the same. Makes no difference when most people living in here don't have typical 9-to-5s. Makes me wonder what the regular schedule and job benefits are for a cartel lieutenant. I make it to her door and knock.

She opens the door. Looks like this time was able to take a shower. A mix of smells of running electronics and a lavender candle or two reaches my nostrils. Lucy sees me, smiles and bites her lower lip. "Come in, come in," she says.

I return the smile and walk inside as I say "alright, alright I'm coming." She closes the door behind me and directs me her sofa and grabs the Oneiros visor to show to me.

"Do it," she says, barely containing her excitement. "We have to know what's in there."

I sigh, for a moment considering if I should mention our former business partner, recently deceased and now probably rotting away in a common grave outside of town. Or reduced to dust. Who knows what they do with unclaimed corpses? Medical testing probably. Now's not the time for sad news. I'm just as curious and excited to see what we caught from the Straya's head.

"Alright, let's do it," I say with a shrug then lie down on the sofa. Lucy is uncharacteristically cheerful as she gently places the Oneiros on my face. "Remember, keep your hands off me," I add.

I hear Lucy let out a giggle then sit in her nerd throne. A few seconds later, everything goes dark and I begin dreaming the diorama of the Maximum Straya.

12

Extracurricular Activities

It's dark and I'm crouching by a tall shrub. I'm… hiding? I look around and see someone else hiding next to me. We're outside, in the woods. Or maybe the Australian outback. Somewhere in the middle of nowhere. The moon and the stars shine brightly in the absence of artificial lighting. Next to our hiding place, there is a dirt trail. I follow it to the left and see it disappear deeper into the woods, then I follow it to the right, beyond the tree line to a clearing far away with several cabins by the edge of a lake. Looks like a typical summer camp.

"Shhh," the guy next to me whispers. "They're almost here." I look at him to see what appears to be a teenager. Probably 15 or 16. He nods towards the distance and I see a couple. A boy and a girl, about the same age. Looks like ToBogan chose the memory of a high school prank to be captured in full catch diorama.

I play along with the scene. I know I'm hiding for some reason, but I don't want to fuck with ToBogan's memory of his younger years. I want to know how it unfolds. I'm also still disturbed by my reaction inside the hobo's diorama. At the time I thought it was his murderous rage driving the scene but later realized that it had all been me. I have to make sure there is no latent asshole murderer inside of my head so this time I figure, I'll just let the diorama unfold to whatever happened here, during the teenager years of the Maximum Straya.

My unnamed partner in crime giggles then whispers "that bitch won't know what hit her. You'll see Topher, you'll see."

Oh shit. This is more than a prank. The couple continues walking towards us and now they're almost on the other side of the shrub. Are we about to mug someone?

The couple eventually walks down the dirt trail toward us, and I see their faces clearly. I know the guy. ToBogan knows him, more like. He's my mate, Todd. We grew up together. I recognize the girl too, her name is Chloe. I asked her out... last week? I remember this place from ToBogan's memory, like if it was my own. This is a Christian retreat in the woods somewhere. It's the Australian Outback alright, but not too far away from civilization. No, just outside town. Just isolated enough for good, upstanding members of the Christian youth group to talk about Jesus. I asked Chloe out and she rejected me. Not only that, she talked to her friends about it. They posted some stupid teenage girl story on the sosh nets. I remember now. It was humiliating. It was infuriating.

Before I realize what's going on, Ollie, who was hiding next to me, jumps out of the shrub and grabs Chloe by the left arm. Todd knows what's going on and now he grabs her by the other. Chloe looks at them and giggles and asks "what the fuck, guys?"

"Come on, dude," Todd says, looking in my general direction. Memories come to me as the scene unfolds.

I follow the memory and stand up, walking out into the clearing so Chloe can see me. She's still giggling, apparently drugged or drunk or both. Chloe recognizes me and asks "Topher?"

I don't say anything, it's what's in the memory. Ollie and Todd grin like idiots. I take a couple steps forward and reach for Chloe's right breast. I give it a good squeeze. Must have been painful, as she looks down then back up at me. Her smile is gone. Through the haze of whatever substance she was given, appears to realize what's going on.

"Topher?" she asks. "What the fuck? Let me go, assholes," she exclaims. Panicking. Her attempts at pulling herself free are vain. After all, she's being held in place by members of the high school rugby team.

I smile, just like ToBogan did in his own memory. I feel like I'm supposed to ask her something, but nothing comes to mind. Maybe way in the back of his mind, before animal instincts took hold, ToBogan wanted to ask why the rejection. No, more like, why the humiliation? Why couldn't she just say no and walk away? Why make him look like a creep online? Topher Bass, captain of the rugby team might have asked these questions and maybe some others but at that point, the animal had taken over. Fascinated, I let the memory unfold. Lucid or not, I let the diorama happen, unaltered, just as things unfolded that warm summer evening when Topher Bass raped his crush.

Without warning, I reach for her dress. Some flimsy thing with floral patterns. Got to make herself look like an innocent little girl to the church people, I guess. I reach for it. I grab and pull. The thing easily tears off. There is no doubt in her mind any longer. She cries, terrified. She understands what's about to happen.

The stupefying haze of full catch diorama mixes my memories and emotions with Topher's. I reach for her bra and rip it off to get a good look at her exposed breasts, dimly but well enough lit by moonlight. Ollie and Todd giggle like hyenas and grab as much skin as they please. There is a part of me recoiling from knowing this is a point of no return. I'll be changed forever and there is no going back after this. But then another looks forward to it in excitement. The animal part. The base instincts of a beast. I don't know which one is mine and which one is Topher's.

From my back pocket, I pull out a small knife. Son of a bitch. ToBogan, not a rapist, but a murderer? Disturbingly relieved that the lesser of two evils prevails, I see myself reach down to cut off and remove her underwear. The girl tries to scream but Todd covers her mouth, so strongly, I see her skin whiten around his hand. She has been struggling for several minutes and now seems out of stamina, just standing there, tears drying out from her face.

"This way," I hear myself whisper.

The boys follow me away from the dirt trail. Not too far from it, we get to a small clearing. There are a couple sleeping bags on the ground. They toss her on them then quickly make sure she doesn't escape by pinning her down.

This was planned in advance. Whatever drug they gave her, the hiding location, the sleeping bags. I know no one is being hurt for real and I know there will be no real consequences. I know that reasoning comes from my own mind, but in Topher's I feel he is also not worried about consequences. I try to remember why and a memory comes to me. A memory about family. His uncle is a high-ranking politician. Someone with power. I can't summon the title exactly, just the image in Topher's head that he is powerful enough to make sure there are no consequences for Topher Bass. Rugby team captain. Prospective heir to a career politician's post. Member of an affluent family. Yeah, the type of guy who never grows up mentally, with daddy and uncle always there to clean up after him. Rich and powerful enough to get away with rape, maybe even murder.

"No…" Chloe whimpers. "No…"

My childhood friends and now partners in crime each grab a leg to separate them and I kneel down and pull out my dick. In their rapey planning, the trio forgot to bring some form of lighting. Maybe for the best, they figured. Less of a chance of anyone catching them in the act. Casually, I pull Todd's and Ollie's hands out of the way. They've been fingering and pinching her genitals, the way a clumsy boy who's only seen porn but never been in the same room with a naked girl would.

I get closer. Much closer. I can taste her ragged breathing. I catch a whiff of her perfume too. Something floral. Sweet. Inviting. Her rejection fucked with me more than it should. Me, I'm rich, I'm the captain of the rugby team. I'm 6.5 foot tall. The fuck else did she want? This could have been a much pleasant experience for her, had she not been a dumb airheaded bitch.

Closer. Much closer. I feel skin touching skin. Chloe trembles and whispers "no…"

No.

Rationality overpowers the animal and I take control of the diorama.

No.

This is a line I can't cross. She's not real. Nothing is real but it disturbs me to the core to even think about reliving ToBogan's hurt ego revenge rape.

No.

I stand and pull my pants up. Ollie looks at me confused then goes "the fuck, bro?"

Todd realizes I'm not going to touch Chloe any further and acts quickly before Ollie beats him to it. He gets on top of her, as he struggles to undo his zipper. They struggle almost comically for a few seconds.

"No," I say. Loudly. The way the rugby captain would. Ollie seems to react to the command and lets go of the girl then stands up, labored breathing and all. But not Todd. Todd is too far gone now. All he cares about is to get his dick wet, one way or another. I get closer and punch his back as hard as I can. Todd moans in pain then falls to the side to lie on his back. Chloe sees an opening and pulls herself up to run away from us, back to the small cluster of summer cabins by the lake. Last I see her, she's running away, naked, crying in panic.

Todd is still on the ground, recoiling in pain. Ollie looks at me for a moment, furious, then charges at me but I'm in control of the diorama. I am Neo the God Damn One up in this bitch. I dodge easily then a shotgun materializes in my hands. I turn and blow Ollie's fucking head off. Todd lies against the base of a tree and cries, as he pathetically shakes his head, peeing himself, begging for his life. Fuck it. Nothing is real anyway. I slowly walk up to him, gently place the end of the barrel in his mouth then pull the trigger. There's blood and brain and skull pieces everywhere. Todd no longer has a head. Blood squirts up from his neck in a way that seems unrealistic.

I let go of the gun, which falls to the forest floor. I could materialize a spaceship or some other nonsensical object but my engineer mind takes over and instead, I settle for testing the limits of the diorama.

A typical passive diorama works much like a classic movie set. Objects, backgrounds and actors form from within the memory of the dreamer when the diorama is caught, but for lucid dioramas, I keep wondering what happens if I take control and move away from the scene captured in dreamer memory. Drenched in blood, little bits of Todd's brain hanging from my shirt, I make my way to the group of cabins by the lake. I look up, down, left, right. Everything looks normal. I feel a gentle early evening breeze run by, fresh with the smells of the nearby lake. It's nighttime but still warm.

As I reach one of the cabins, I notice it. The hole. An absence of... things. There is a void, away in the distance, on the right. I figured reaching the end of the 'stage' would be much like bugging one's character out of map boundaries in a videogame. One would see the empty backs of building, cars and whatever objects seen from an angle not meant to be seen. But it is not the case for full catch diorama. It's not even like a black hole. Doesn't feel like the edge of an island. It's more like a boundary where reality ends. I don't even see it. It just feels wrong. Just looking in that direction causes discomfort in my eyes, a slight headache. It's as if my mind struggles to interpret what my eyes are seeing and what I end up perceiving is a fog, extending from the ground up to the sky, as far as I can see.

I keep walking to the cabins. There are four of them, arranged so their doors all face the center of the clearing where there is a campfire. No one's around that I can see or hear. Not even the panicked Chloe running here naked, escaping her would-be rapists. All by myself, I figure I'll test if there is a time limit to the diorama. These are usually set in post-production, when unnecessary moments caught need to be removed so the experience falls within the comfortable half-hour block. I sit by the campfire and grab one of the sticks with a marshmallow on it I find lying around. I hold it close to the fire and it roasts immediately I've always found roasted marshmallows incredibly disgusting to smell or taste. I still don't understand why people eat them. I catch a whiff of the smell and gag in disgust. I toss the thing away from me.

There is no rush. I sit there, reflecting on the fact ToBogan's full catch diorama is probably going to make us very rich. There is virality potential here. A scandalous, embarrassing sexual thing from a somewhat established celebrity. Just have to find a way to publish it without his knowledge. Maybe we'll tell him this catch failed and we need to get another one. We publish both under different merchant names in the darkweb. He'll suspect but won't be able to prove it was us.

Yeah the money will be good. Still bothers me, both times I took control of a full catch diorama ended up in a homicidal rampage. Maybe I do have some kind of serial killer thing inside of me. Maybe bringing it out safely in dreaming these lucid dioramas is going to be therapeutic. Got to make sure we find a way to market them as therapy. 'Face your demons and conquer them,' or some similar bullshit tagline.

An hour or so goes by. Although the scene is frozen in time. The sun is still halfway visible over mountain ranges in the distance. The temperature hasn't changed. Looks like the time of day will stay as it was in dreamer memory. I figure there is no point in staying here. But before I leave, I want to test the limits of the diorama stage again. I stand up and take a quick glance at the four cabins. By their doors, there are cute wooden signs with hand-painted lettering. One for boys, one for girls, one for counselors and the last, unmarked, maybe meant as a common hall of sorts. I walk towards the second one, its door tagged 'Girls'. I doubt the Maximum Straya ever set foot inside. There is no way he knows what's inside in his memories. I open the door and replacing it, blocking the way inside, there is a foggy wall, just like the one marking the border between the stage and the void.

I reach for it and my hand goes through but then hits a solid object beyond the fog where I can't see. I try with my other hand, same results. I push with both, nothing happens. Screw it, what's the worst that could happen? I simply walk through the fog and I feel a force pulling me inside suddenly, then the usual feeling of reality warping overwhelms my senses as I get ejected from full catch diorama.

13

The Dream Is Over

I wake up from dreaming the rapey teenage adventures of the Maximum Straya. There's not much time to fully recover, as soon as I take off the Oneiros, I see Lucy standing next to me, arms crossed, her face indicating she's about to break into tears.

"What's going on?" I ask, voice slurred.

Without an answer, she points to her computer monitor where I see news helicopter footage of an expensive-looking condo building in... Santa Monica? The news alert on the bottom of the screen scrolls past, notifying me of the mysterious and sudden death of a certain Australian rama celebrity.

"Fuck," I think out loud without noticing. "Just like the hobo."

"What?" Lucy asks, half-screaming. "You knew this was going to happen?"

"Okay, calm down," I say, focusing on her, as I stand up, stumbling about as I try to regain my balance.

"Don't tell me to fucking calm down!" Oh yeah, not a good idea to suggest a near hysterical woman to calm down. "It's your dreamcatcher, you killed them."

"Look, it could be a coincidence. Have they announced the cause of death?"

"Coincidence? How stupid do you think I am?" she walks near her desk, tears flowing out of her eyes, pointing at the 'Breaking News' notice on it. It outlines early examination of ToBogan's body exhibits sudden central nervous system failure. Cascading hemorrhages all over the brain. Some sort of massive brain-wide aneurysm. Medical examiners have no idea how it happened. "Is that good enough of a coincidence?"

"Listen, Lucy," I say, making my voice a bit deeper than normal, maybe that will get my point across. "He was just some vapid celebrity from the bunch, who cares? The rama we caught from him, shows he gang-raped some girl that rejected him in high school, the guy was a fucking asshole."

Lucy covers her mouth and tries to wipe tears at the same time. She looks at me like I'm sort of serial killer and she's the next victim. "So that's good enough excuse to kill him?" she asks, voice trembling.

"I didn't know it was going to happen when we caught the diorama," I defend myself. "I only found out about the hobo last night after I dropped off ToBogan."

"His name was Topher," she says, almost whispering.

I sigh and look down, massaging my temples. How can I make her understand the scandalous nature of the rama is going to go viral instantly, especially if he just died. This is the perfect storm of virality and she refuses to see it.

"Look, I'm very sorry he's dead," I say, lowering my voice. Must sound as non-threatening as possible. "You have to see what's in the diorama. He was no Aussie angel. It will go viral very fast. This is the break we needed to get our company to stand out from the crowd."

"Money really is all you care about."

"No… well yes," I say, at least I should be honest. "But there's also us." I approach and touch her shoulder. She flinches away like a scared kitten. "I'm hardware, you're software remember? We're going to make it big, remember?"

She sobs harder now. "Not like this," she manages to mutter.

I don't have time for pointless melodrama. She'll see what I mean when she's out of her hysterical fit. I gently push her aside and sit in her nerd throne. With a few clicks, the one and only full catch diorama of the now deceased Topher Bass goes out into the wild of the darknets. I turn the chair around. Lucy stands there, holding her smartphone so I can see the screen.

There is a connected call to 911.

Fuck. Me. I look her in the eyes and shake my head in disappointment, before I turn the chair back and type a new password for the admin portal of our diorama marketplace. My diorama marketplace. My idea. My genius. Fuck her, I don't need her. I stand up from the chair. The 911 call has been going on for about 5 minutes and neither of us has spoken. The cops are probably on their way, if not already outside. I make for the door and hold it open, for a moment turning back to look at her. Lucy. Former girlfriend. Former fuck buddy. Former business partner. I feel like I should say something deep and grand to mark the end of our relationship, but nothing comes to mind. I sigh again and close the door behind me.

Sunlight burns my retinas and I close my eyes to block the onslaught. I'm outside of Lucy's building. I stop myself before I walk back to my car. Built-in GPS and motion tracking will make it easy for them to find me. Fuck. I pull out my smartphone and turn it off. Maybe some latent GPS tracking remains even in power-saving mode. No electronic device is truly powered off ever nowadays. So, I say goodbye to my connection to the world and hurl it as hard as

I can into the apartment building across the street. After a second, I hear a mild splash. It hit the pool. Lucky shot. Wait, never mind. The fucking thing is waterproof.

It's going to be a long walk to my place. Better now than never. I check my wallet. I have a couple hundred bucks in cash. Somehow, I always knew there would be a point in my life where I wouldn't be able to rely on credit cards or any other electronic forms of payment. Can't pay for a ride without one though. Can't flag down an Uber and just offer cash. Long walk it is.

*

The sun sets as I reach my neighborhood. Downtown LA. Once home and workplace to very wealthy, very powerful entertainment, sports, banking and industry captains, assorted celebrities and whoever else rich enough to pay $10k a month for a one bedroom cuck box. Nowadays a cesspool of bused-over homeless people. A huge mass of a mix of the economically disenfranchised, the mentally ill and the substance addicted. My plump physique is not built for this kind of commitment to walking. I can barely stand the rashes in between my fat folds. Makes me walk around like a penguin.

It's been several hours now since I left Lucy's place. ToBogan's death is so high-profile they're probably looking for me all over the place. I turn the corner towards my building, and just like I guessed, I see a black car parked a few spaces away from the door. Two occupants inside. Plain-clothes police. Away, towards the building across the street, I see a uniformed police walk away then turn the corner. Stationed there in case I run away, I guess.

Where to go? I look west towards Staples Center, then east. That's it! The underground, multilevel tent city of Pershing Square. Takes me longer than it should to reach the rusted-shut escalators down to the first sublevel. Can barely walk now. The strong smell of fresh fecal matter hits me like a truck as I walk down the once-powered automatic escalators. Looking down to watch my step in the darkness underground, I find the source of the smell. Smeared shit on the steel walls of the narrow escalators. I climb down carefully. It's my first night as a homeless person but I still have my dignity.

The ground level was little indicator of what was going on down here. The first sublevel, a former underground parking lot is now tightly packed with a fetid mass of unwashed humanity. Some small tents scattered here and there and blankets hanging from strings tied to concrete columns provide some degree of privacy for some of the occupants. Empty oil barrels here and there burn trash for light and heat. Makes me wonder how the lot of crazies and druggies hasn't died from CO_2 poisoning. Smoke probably exits out the passive vent system that back in the day extracted car emissions.

Should be close to midnight now, but there seems to be no ordinary day and night cycles in here. There is no sunlight making it down. No way to tell the passage of time. And the people down here are probably too far gone to care about a 24-hour schedule. I thought people would be asleep by now but instead, the place is lively with the grunts and moans and crying of the mentally fucked up. I walk the small walkways in between rows of stinky people. I see drug trades going on. I see prostitutes trading filled needles for blowjobs. Some of them young enough someone should be tucking them in bed for the night instead.

Several orange lunch boxes lie on the floor. I kick one of them and see the logo of one of the non-profits outside. There are no showers or bathrooms or much privacy down here but at least I'll have something to eat in the morning. I'm exhausted. Lost count of how many miles I walked today. Should be safe here. Police can't go near a hobo by law. They can't come down here. Somehow, I manage to find a little space by the far wall. I sit down. I lie down. Wondering if a crazy hobo will slit my throat in my sleep for taking their spot, I doze off.

*

It's been three days. I think. I count the days by how many times I've gone to sleep after several hours of sitting in this spot, too fearful of losing it to a new resident of the homeless ecosystem. Luckily, non-profit volunteers come down a couple times every so many hours with carts full of orange-boxed meals. I've even gotten some spare needles. Not like I'm going to use them but I still hold on to them. Might come in handy, if my suspicions of them being used as ad hoc currency in this underworld are true.

I remember there used to be a gag-inducing smell. A fetid emulsion of feces, urine and semen. But after three days in the warm, damp protection of this underground parking lot, I detect nothing. My senses have gotten used to their new home. All I can smell is a sort of damp earth. Not even the constant murmuring and the noises of the crazies going about their self-awareness free existences bothers me. Maybe I'll stay down here. It's somewhat cozy. Not having to worry about the police or paying taxes. I can see now why some choose the lifestyle. Yeah, maybe I'll find a mate down here. We'll have sooth-covered children. We'll raise them to be upstanding members of the tent city society. Yeah, this is where I find happiness, Among the shit, empty needles, filled condoms and dried piss.

*

Its' been... uhhh... 2 weeks? Give or take a couple days. I've learned to understand the microcosmos down here. Made a friend. Scotty was his name. Shared some of his heroin a couple days ago. I had never done drugs before. Just not my thing. But Scotty gave me a low dosage, entry level. Maybe Scotty was feeling generous or maybe he wanted to get me hooked up. One more junkie to sustain the tent city economy. The high came and went. Haven't seen Scotty ever since. I know how these things fuck with your pleasure receptors in the brain bit I still want more. I want the high again. I just have to ignore the need and it will go away before I'm lost to it. I hope it goes away.

Scotty also mentioned who runs this place. A local cartel representative that goes by '*El Talegas*.' Between giggles, Scotty translated the nickname to 'The Scrotum' or 'The Testicles'. Makes one wonder how Mexican cartel officers keep straight faces when addressing each other with such names. Or how the nicknames came to be to begin with. Supposedly *El Talegas* has an office down in the 4th sublevel. All the way down there, shielded from police interference, just like I though.

A non-profit dude left an orange meal box next to me while I was passed out. So hungry. I open the box and find a turkey sandwich, orange juice, napkins, utensils and an alcohol wipe. I devour the whole thing within seconds. Well, except for the inedibles, of course. I wipe my hands clean with the wet towelette.

My whole body aches. Between grunts and out loud swearing, I manage to sit up. No way I can stand up, with my brain still so fucked up. I touch my face. I find 2 weeks' worth of unkempt facial hairs and a goop composed of layers of dried-up sweat mixed with dirt. Between crawling and holding on to a wall, I make it a few feet to the row of buckets where hobos shit in the open. Luckily the overflowed ones have been switched by a nonprofit or another one. The first few days, I was too self-conscious to relieve myself in front of others but by now, all dignity is gone. Plus it's such a common sight, no one cares to stare at the fat guy taking a shit. No wonder my spot was empty and no one has claimed or attempted to take it from me. It's just too close to the shit buckets. I guess even some hobos have standards.

I do the crawling on all fours trip back to my spot and lie down. I'll need a couple more days to purge the substance out of my brain.

*

A few days ago, I came up with a plan to get out of here. These cartel types have all kinds of resources. I'm sure they wouldn't mind carrying a gringo out of the US, across the border. I could then somehow make it through Mexico, past Central America and down to Brazil or Venezuela. I think those two don't have extradition treaties with the US. I just have to somehow get my life savings out of the bank to pay for it. I'm a fugitive now, my accounts are probably frozen. But these cartel types surely have the resources to get that money out too.

I stood up and said good-bye to the filthy piece of floor that was my bed and dwelling for the last few days. Dirt and sweat have caked underneath filthy clothes. I feel the dried crust grind to dust as I walk down to the second sublevel. It's not so much different from the first. The next one is about the same. Eventually, I make it to the 4th sublevel. Ventilation is not as good. It's hotter too. It's like a damp sauna, shit particles floating in the air. Untold bacteria and filth enter my body as I breathe in. Beyond the escalators, on the other side of the wall, I see a section of the sublevel that has been walled off with pieces of steel containers. It's anyone's guess how the huge panels were brought in. Probably stolen from the abandoned port of San Pedro, cut to specification and lowered with sidewalk elevators. Thick, strong steel that would withstand most firearm calibers. The perfect fortress for a last stand, in the event police was allowed by the city to storm the place.

Around the corner where steel walls meet, there is a door, cut into the container panels. Two *amigos* stand in guard. They wear pointy snakeskin boots, expensive-looking jeans and button-up shirts and even white-pearl cowboy hats. Who wears cowboy hats underground? I walk up to them and they stare me down. Might as well try and break the ice.

"Hello, friendos," I say, voice slurred and legs trembling from the effort. The two cartel soldiers look at me stone-faced, then at each other, then back at me. The one on the right walks up to me and faster than I can react to, punches me in the gut. I bend over then fall to my knees, struggling to breathe so I don't pass out.

It takes considerable effort to recover well enough to look up and see the cartel soldier who punched me squeezing a hand sanitizer packet in his hands. His friend, arms crossed, motions away with his head and says *"orale, a la verga puto gringo."*

I only understand the last word, but I don't really need to know ghetto Spanish to know I'm being told to fuck off. At least I'm being allowed to walk away with my head still attached to my neck. How nice of them. I nod and get up then somehow manage to walk away. I don't make it all the way to the broken-down escalator to the third sublevel when I hear slurred giggling behind me. I turn and see Scotty. He's an ancient-looking dude who wears a wifebeater, which covers about half of his pot belly, a filthy pair of jean shorts and plastic surfer sandals. No doubt freebies from the non-profit's pile outside.

Scotty walks up to me laughing then hits me in the back, real hard, I have to tense my muscles to stay upright then says, voice coarse from smoking one herb or another, "you wanted blow why didn't you come to me, friend?"

"No," I mutter then gasp for air. I can't finish my sentence and shake my head instead. Scotty laughs again, loudly, then leads me away from the escalator to a pile of cardboard boxes where he sits down and motions for me to follow. Stumbling about, I do.

"What are you doing down here, dude?" Scotty asks, way too close to me. The stink of rotten teeth wakes me the fuck up.

"*Talegas...*" I mutter. "I have to talk to the boss man."

My companion with the assortment of months-fermented bodily odors snorts and lets out thunderous laughter. "No way, Jose. Only way to see *El Talegas* is if you have business with the Cartel or if you're about to be cooked alive inside an oil barrel."

"Help me," I say, mustering energy from who knows where. "I want to buy my way out of the US. I need to make it to Mexico."

"Ah," Scotty says, uncharacteristically serious. "Man on the run, I see."

No answer from me besides a nod in acknowledgement. No need to get into specifics.

"How much you got?" he asks, getting even closer to me. I can see the black gaps in between meth-melted teeth. Like I'm going to tell him.

"That's for *El Talegas* to know," I say.

Scotty goes back to his former merry self and explodes in laughter. From that close, I feel my ears ringing from it. "That's fine, keep your secrets," he says, nodding. "Let me see what I can do for you."

My new friend stands up and walks towards the men with the snakeskin boots. I doubt they're going to listen to him. In fact, I pay attention to the scene to watch them kick the shit out of him. But he talks, and laughs and motions to them, then points back at me. The cartel soldiers stare at him, then at each other, then back at him. But there is no ass kicking. Instead, one of them says something in Spanish and motions to Scotty to get away from them. Well, at least he tried. Scotty pulls up his loose jean shorts to cover his ass crack and waves and laughs as he makes his way to me.

"I told you, it's all good," he says, as he sits back next to me.

"What do you mean?"

"You sit here and wait your turn, they'll come get you when *El Talegas* is ready to see you."

"Really?" I ask, incredulous. "That was easy."

My pot-bellied friend laughs loudly then says "*amigo, down here I'm the top sales dog. You got any idea how much these guys make through me, peddling their fine wares? I got pull with these guys, you see.*"

"If you say so," I say, rubbing the mouth of my stomach, wishing I had found Scotty before I attempted reasoning with the bad *hombres*.

We sit there for what feel like hours. Scotty tells me stories about his time in the Marines, guarding poppy flower fields in Afghanistan and I mostly ignore him, waiting for the cartel soldiers to call my number. Or my name. Or whatever. But they haven't moved from their spot. Not since I got punched. How are they going to tell Mr. *Talegas* that I'm waiting for an audience? At some point, Scotty excuses himself and gets up, maybe to go sell some more drugs or maybe to use the shit bucket. His words slur past me and I forget immediately. I haven't eaten anything in over a day. I guess the non-profits chefs don't venture all the way down here with the lunch boxes. So weak. So sleepy.

*

There's a loud clap and a stinging pain on my face and I'm woken up by Mr. Pointy Boots with a hard slap. I become fully alert within a second and stand up to see him crush another hand sanitizer packet between his hands. His friend motions with his head towards the door in the back and says "*orale, vamonos, pinche gringo puto.*" Again, I only understand the last word but I get it, I'm being escorted into the inner lair of *El Talegas*.

120

14

Unexpected Acquaintances

Behind the steel door, I find what looks like a poorly lit breakroom. Seems to be a sort of common hall, with some other doors in the far walls, maybe leading to Cartel narco tunnels, or maybe backdoors for the men with the pointy snakeskin boots to come and go without having to suffer the indignity of walking by the unwashed mass of homeless humanity.

There are several tables and chairs. Discarded fast food containers, empty soda bottles. Against the walls by the door we came in, there are a few tables with coffee machines, disposable cups and so on. I even spot a big box of hand sanitizer packets, like the ones used by the cartel soldier. The guy leading me in pushes hard enough that I almost lose my balance, but I somehow keep myself from falling on my face. I turn around and see them standing guard by the door, each holds a shiny handgun with arms down in front. The cartel soldier on the left holds a silver-plated gun, the one on the right is gold-plated. They both have intricate patterns of skulls, smaller guns and what seems to be some sort of

121

female skeletal deity. Silver-plated gun guy waves with his hand for me to get away from them. I nod and obey.

I take a few steps into the center of the room. It's still kind of dark, I stumble upon a chair and hit my pinkie toe on its steel frame. Fuck, it hurts, but I don't let it show. Before I continue further in, I notice a third cowboy-hat-wearing person sitting at a table. He's eating a taco. There is a Corona beer next to his plate. I figure this is my host, the illustrious *Señor Talegas*. I get closer to him. There are several chairs around me but choose to stand, until told otherwise. So I stand there while the short, chubby, brown skinned man with a Hitler-like mustache enjoys his snack.

The man looks up to take a glance at me for a second, then down to continue working the massive taco into his mouth. I'm not one for Mexican food but I haven't eaten in over a day. I wish Mr. *Talegas* would share.

"So you want to cross the border," my chubby friend asks, heavy accent and all, never looking away from his plate. It's got black refried beans, rice and sour cream. I notice a slice of avocado too.

"Uhu…" I mutter. Saliva fills my mouth. No choice but to swallow it.

"It's going to cost you," he says, looking at me, then grabbing the Corona to take a sip.

"I have money," I say, shaking from hunger. "Just have to figure out how to get it out of the bank."

The chubby man who hasn't actually introduced himself nods, wiping his hands with a dirty napkin. "And therein lies your predicament," he says. Sounds like Shakespeare being narrated by a Mexican peasant. "I dare say, my friend, you may not wish to agree to the cost."

"Huh…" I mumble. The fat man nods again and picks up a second taco then takes a bite off it. Somehow half of the huge thing is gone.

No other choice but to stand there awkwardly as he chews patiently. After a couple minutes, he washes the taco down with a sip of Corona then says, "you want to talk to *El Talegas*."

"Huh... I thought you were *El Talegas*."

The unnamed chubby guy chuckles and shakes his head as he says, apparently to himself, "*pinche gringo pendejo*."

I understood the second word. "So, when can I see this Mr. *Talegas*?"

Without answering, the fat Mexican signals with his head behind him. I see two men walking through one of the doors in the back, then towards us. White men. Men wearing expensive-looking suits. The one leading reaches the table and talks with the chubby Mexican in fluent Spanish. They both look at me and stare me up and down then laugh loudly. In between words I can understand things like '*gringo*', '*puto*' and '*pendejo*'. Just what the fuck is going on?

"Alright then," says the leading man. White, blonde hair, black eyes. Body language that indicates he owns the place.

Mr. Chubby Mustache nods and stands up. He grabs the empty plate and walks away. He meets the two soldiers with the snakeskin boots then they all leave the break room. Mysterious suit #2 stands there in the distance, while Blonde Suit grabs a chair and sits down.

"Go on, sit down," he says. I immediately comply. We're now sitting right in front of each other. Mr. Blonde suits rests his hands on his lap, legs crossed way too tightly. Tight enough to crush a man's balls. It's an oddly effeminate way of sitting but other than that, the man exudes full composure. Full power.

We sort of stare at each other in silence for a couple minutes. Got to break the ice, so I ask "you're *El Taleg-*"

"Theodore Davis," he interrupts, voice like a small thunder. "Rents an apartment at 780 Figueroa, former Dreamax employee, random easily replaceable IT guy. Stole an expensive piece of equipment..."

"Allegedly," I clarify.

The man that supposedly goes by *El Talegas* glares at me in a way that discourages further interruptions, then casually ignoring my comment continues by saying "…with which he built a custom diorama catching apparatus that not only catches an interactive, or 'lucid' diorama as he calls them in his Tor marketplace, but kills the user shortly after."

What the fuck? He knows everything. "What the fuck?"

The blonde suit scoffs then shakes his head with a giggle that sounds as if coming out from a small foghorn. "You stupid fucking simpleton," he says.

"Hey," I say, in vain attempting to defend my dignity.

Mr. *Talegas* interrupts and says "what, you thought you'd be safe selling your smut on Tor?"

How the fuck? No point in answering the question.

"You dumb motherfucker," Mr. *Talegas* chuckles then turns to look at his similarly suited partner standing behind him and asks "isn't he a dumb motherfucker, Mr. Jefferson?"

"Dumb motherfucker indeed, Mr. Hancock," replies Jefferson, arms crossed, permanent expression in his face like he recently caught a whiff of a silent fart.

Jefferson. Hancock. Obviously not their real names.

"Do you know why you are a dumb motherfucker, Mr. Davis?" asks *El Talegas*, also known as Mr. Hancock, whatever his real name is.

"Hummm," I mumble before being interrupted again by the enigmatic suit.

"Because Tor was made by the US Navy, commissioned for by an intelligence agency or another," explains Mr. Jefferson, condescending tone never under control. "An encrypted anonymous Internet routing network, supposedly gives you online anonymity," he ends the comment with a chuckle. Mr. Jefferson behind chuckles too. "How anonymous do you think you are if I have access to the Tor root encryption keys?"

My turn to chuckle, then say "yeah right. I know all that, to have root keys you'd need to be NSA or CI…" Fuck.

"Now he gets it, doesn't he, Mr. Jefferson?" The other suit nods in agreement.

"You guys are NSA."

"Well," says Mr. Hancock, "we're something or other. I don't know, shit changes all the time."

"Huh…" I mumble. "So you can help me get out of the country?"

This is apparently very humorous to Mr. Hancock, who laughs for a few seconds. He regains his composure then says "there is a warrant for your arrest out there, you retarded waste of oxygen," abandoning the effeminate sitting stance, instead leaning towards me, elbows on knees, hands held together. "Two counts of premeditated manslaughter, one count assault of an individual experiencing homelessness, one count assault of an individual named Lucia Cortez and one count theft of Dreamax property. Well, this is California so you don't have to worry about death penalty but for sure you're going away for a long time."

"So you're here to take me in?"

Mr. Hancock shakes his head with a smile then reclines back on his chair. "You have any idea how much they pay me? Why would someone like me bother with a random criminal like you? I'm beginning to think your mother used to do cocaine when she was pregnant with you, and then made it a habit of dropping you on your head as a baby."

"Humm," I mumble again. Between being halfway starved to death, dizzy from my own body odor due to not having showered in what feels has been a month and the confusion over just what the fuck is going on, I don't have the energy to figure out what this asshole is going on about. I just sit there in silence.

"Stupid numb skull doesn't even know this is his lucky day," says Mr. Hancock. Mr. Jefferson chuckles behind him. "No Mr. Davis, I'm here to tell you we're going to make all these charges go away."

The shock from hearing this wakes me out of the haze of malnutrition.

"Yeah, you liked hearing that, didn't you?"

"No, it's just," I say, voice trembling from weakness. "How can you do that? Why would you do that?"

"Oh, let's just say we have the right friends in the right places," Mr. Hancock explains himself, smug smile on his face. "Some of these friends believe there is certain value to these full catch dioramas of yours. Do you want to be our friend too?"

"Yeah," I say without giving it much thought. I can go back to my life. I can take a shower again.

"As to why, well, it will become apparent very soon."

For a few minutes I consider the fact I may be signing a deal with the devil. Maybe I died from heroin overdose and this is the actual devil fucking with me. I mean, '*El Talegas*'? Come on. I then ask "what about Topher Bass' death? That's pretty high profile."

Without an answer, Mr. Hancock pulls out a smartphone from his jacket, unlocks then fiddles with it for a while. Eventually, he presents the screen to me. I know this, it's the administrator portal to Lucy's... errr, my Tor showcase website. He browses to the statistics page where I see there have been 2.6 billion unique downloads worldwide. ToBogan's diorama has gone insanely viral. At 99 cents per download...

"I'm a billionaire," I say stupidly.

"Indeed," says Mr. Hancock, then pockets back his smartphone. I choose not to ask how he knows the login password to my highly encrypted Tor website. "the idiot masses out there are more concerned with reliving Mr. Bass' teenage raping adventures than asking themselves how he died. He's been marked as an undesirable so now no one gives a single fuck about the circumstances of his death."

"I see," I say. "So, I get to keep that money?"

"Pocket change in the grand scheme of things, it is of no consequence to us," replies Mr. Hancock.

"What about the Dreamax... thing? What about the homeless dude?"

"You still don't seem to understand we have the resources to sweep such minor things under the rug," Mr. Hancock answers, now more arrogantly than ever. "Besides, we have a scapegoat." It appears the suits decide this is the end of the conversation. Mr. Hancock gets up and adjusts his expensive-looking suit. "Go home, Mr. Davis. Take a shower, jerk off, sleep, do whatever the hell you normally do. We'll be in touch."

I can't believe this. I'm free. I'm a billionaire. It's all good except for a small detail. "Who's the scapegoat?" I ask.

Mr. Hancock answers as he walks to the same door they came in. "Why Lucia Cortez, of course."

"What? No!" I exclaim, standing up.

The suits stop and Mr. Hancock turns, as he sighs in annoyance, having to explain things. "Let's just say Ms. Cortez lacks the entrepreneurial spirit required to lead the diorama empire we envision."

Diorama empire. I like those two words being that close together. Lucy overreacted and called the cops on me and she's the one going to jail? I'll get over it.

Without further explanation, the two suits exit the room and I'm left there by myself. I look around but don't see anyone. Fuck it, I'm too hungry. I go scavenging for food at the tables by the microwave ovens and find several popcorn packets. I prepare one. Usually, I hate this salty crap, kernel pieces sticking between my teeth but I'm too hungry to care about being picky. The packet finishes cooking, I get it out of the over, open it and eat. Jesus Christ, sweet holy nectar of the gods.

I'm munching tongue-burning popcorn when I see the two cartel soldiers approach. They talk to each other, pointing at me. I understand 'gringo' and 'puto'. One of them gets closer, rudely grabs the popcorn bag from my hand and throws it aside.

"Hey," I say, as best as one can with a mouthful of popcorn. "I was eating that."

"*Orale, pinche gringo*," says snakeskin boots cowboy number 2. "*Vamonos, a la verga.*"

A la verga it is and so I'm led to the staircase up the next sublevel of the hell on earth that is the Pershing Square tent city. I climb staircases up 4 stories laboriously. I note how the higher I get, the less hellish the former subterranean parking lot gets.

Finally, I make it outside. I hadn't seen sunlight in... a month? Where before driving by with windows down was a gag-inducing experience, now the air feels clean, compared to the concentrated cocktail of festering bodily odors underground. I take a step off the broken-down escalator and look around, I see the business of homelessness go about as usual. The mentally fucked up laughing or yelling incoherently. The well-meaning NGO and non-profit employees go around distributing food, clean needles and used clothes to the residents of the tent city. Portable diorama visors too, the cheap stuff, paid for with tax money.

And I'm a billionaire.

A technology entrepreneur. A trailblazer. A captain of industry.

15

Captain of Industry

Six months later.

"You imbecile sack of shit," says Mr. Hancock over speakerphone. Good thing the glass doors to the office of the CEO, my office, are well insulated for noise. Wouldn't want the troops outside hear how the suits talk to me.

"Excuse me," I say, in a likely vain attempt to regain a sliver of dignity. "Can you go one sentence without calling me something horrible?"

I hear Mr. Hancock scoff then he continues, "like I said, you retarded waste of oxygen, we have friends who will make sure the bill passes in Texas. After that, California will follow suit. Before you know it, the whole god damn thing will go national."

"I still think it's a bit unethical to catch full dioramas off death row inmates," I say.

"Oh boo-hoo, cry me a river. Look at all the money only two ramas have made you in the last 6 months. Once you are legally allowed to start catching the really fucked up shit from murderers and other scum of the earth like you, then you'll have your empire."

"Yeah... I guess," I say. Should be wiping my tears of social justice outrage with $100 bills.

"How's the content injection project working out?"

"The technical problems can be worked around," I say. Again, something inside pushes to come out, against all self-preservation and profit-making instincts. "It's just that... we'll be basically injecting err... subliminal messages? I'm not comfortable with my dioramas having what is basically mind control code."

"Oh for fucks sakes, they're advertisements. Everyone does a native ad every now and then why shouldn't you?"

I don't have a counter argument. He's right, it wouldn't be any different from TV show commercial breaks back in the day. But we're better than that. Here at Full Catch Diorama, the hottest new technology startup, we inject the ad directly in the content, so there are no commercial breaks, which would interrupt the immersion of the experience. Yeah, we're pioneering technology here. We're trailblazers. Innovators. And we're going to change the world.

"Keep an eye out for the Texas vote tomorrow," Mr. Hancock continues his list of tasks assigned to me. "As soon as you hear of a yay majority, get your ass down there. I'll build a list of upcoming executions while you travel."

Catching a dreamer-killing full diorama will still be illegal in the rest of the country but distributing it will not. Mr. Hancock's friends in Congress are very persuasive indeed.

"Will do," I say. Without any further comments, he hangs up. We're about to make history. Music, videogames, VR, traditional dioramas. All things of the past.

My computer screen displays the news for the day. Lucy's trial starts in six months. Somehow Mr. Hancock and his friends in powerful places got the attorney general to shift the two manslaughter charges on her. After all, she was the one who wrote the code that killed the two unfortunate test subjects. I was an accessory to crimes I was not aware of at the time. She's facing life in prison while I sit here, in the CEO office of a technology startup valued at 282 billion dollars. Why did she have to call 911? We could be celebrating together right now.

I grab my bottle of Hetap Reserve from the desk and take a sip. $1000 a bottle, huh? Fuck, I fell for the native ad. Doesn't even taste anything special.

About the Author

Nick Salomon is a nobody. He is not a celebrity, nor a friend or family of anyone in the entertainment industries. Nick is not connected to anyone who matters in the book publishing world. He did not kiss the right asses in college. Hell, his major was not even English.

In so many words, Nick Salomon is an outsider who does not belong to any of the tight nepotistic milieus that matter for one to get their written work published.

Nick never underwent any formal training in fiction writing, nor did he earn any accolades or favorable critic reviews.

Nick is more of a random guy who observes the world around him through a very cynical lens, then writes down whatever comes to mind as a hobby. Occasionally, this produces a short story, or if lucky, a novel.

Nick lives in Los Angeles, California, which explains his hopeless contempt for humanity.

nick.salomon@blueben.ch